T0200909

'I love reading Simenon. He makes me think of Chekhov'
– William Faulkner

'A truly wonderful writer . . . marvellously readable – lucid, simple, absolutely in tune with the world he creates'
– Muriel Spark

'Few writers have ever conveyed with such a sure touch, the bleakness of human life' – A. N. Wilson

'One of the greatest writers of the twentieth century . . . Simenon was unequalled at making us look inside, though the ability was masked by his brilliance at absorbing us obsessively in his stories' – *Guardian*

'A novelist who entered his fictional world as if he were part of it' – Peter Ackroyd

'The greatest of all, the most genuine novelist we have had in literature' – André Gide

'Superb . . . The most addictive of writers . . . A unique teller of tales' – *Observer*

'The mysteries of the human personality are revealed in all their disconcerting complexity' – Anita Brookner

'A writer who, more than any other crime novelist, combined a high literary reputation with popular appeal'
– P. D. James

'A supreme writer . . . Unforgettable vividness'– *Independent*

'Compelling, remorseless, brilliant' – *John Gray*

'Extraordinary masterpieces of the twentieth century'
– John Banville

GEORGES SIMENON

Maigret's Memoirs

Translated by HOWARD CURTIS

PENGUIN BOOKS

PENGUIN CLASSICS

UK | USA | Canada | Ireland | Australia
India | New Zealand | South Africa

Penguin Books is part of the Penguin Random House group of companies
whose addresses can be found at global.penguinrandomhouse.com

Penguin
Random House
UK

First published in French as *Les mémoires de Maigret* by Presses de la Cité 1951
This translation first published 2016

010

Set in Dante MT Std 12.5/15pt
Typeset in India by Thomson Digital Pvt Ltd, Noida, Delhi
Printed and bound in Great Britain by Clays Ltd, Elcograf S.p.A.

ISBN: 978-0-241-24017-5

www.greenpenguin.co.uk

Maigret's Memoirs

1.

In which I am not displeased to have the opportunity to at last say something about my relations with a man named Simenon

It was in 1927 or 1928. I have no memory for dates, and I am not one of those people who carefully keep written records of everything they do: a not uncommon activity in our profession, and one that has proved quite useful to some, even occasionally profitable. And it is only quite recently that I remembered the exercise books into which my wife – for quite a long time without my knowing it, and even on the sly – stuck press cuttings about me.

Because of a particular case that caused us some difficulty that year . . . I could probably find the exact date, but I do not have the courage to start rummaging among those exercise books.

Not that it matters. When it comes to the weather, on the other hand, my memories are very clear. It was a nondescript day at the beginning of winter, one of those colourless days, in grey and white, the kind I am tempted to call an administrative day, because you have the impression that nothing interesting can happen in such a dull atmosphere and you are so bored that all you want to do in the office is bring files up to date, finish off reports that have been lying around for a long time, and determinedly but half-heartedly dispose of day-to-day work.

The only reason I insist on this greyness, this flatness, is not out of a taste for the picturesque, but to show how banal the thing was in itself, swamped by the unremarkable events of an ordinary day.

It was about ten in the morning. The daily report had been over for nearly half an hour, having been a short one.

Even the least informed members of the public now know more or less what the Police Judiciaire's daily report consists of, but at that time, most Parisians would have been hard put to say even what offices were housed at the Quai des Orfèvres.

On the dot of nine, a bell summons the various heads of department to the commissioner's large office, whose windows look out over the Seine. There is nothing grand about the meeting. We go to it smoking our pipes or cigarettes, usually with files under our arms. The day has not yet got into gear and there is still a vague whiff of coffee and croissants in the air. We shake hands. We chat idly while waiting for everybody to arrive.

Then we take turns bringing the chief up to date on what has been happening in our departments. Some remain standing, sometimes at the window, watching the buses and taxis crossing the Pont Saint-Michel.

Contrary to what the public may imagine, the talk is not only about criminals. 'How's your daughter, Priollet? Is she over her measles?'

I even remember hearing cooking recipes explained in some detail.

We talk about more serious things too, obviously. About a deputy's or minister's son, for example, who has been getting into all kinds of trouble, seems unable to stop himself doing so, and needs to be reined in urgently before there is a scandal. Or else a wealthy foreigner who has recently been staying in a luxury hotel on the Champs-Élysées and about whom the government is starting to get worried. Or a little girl found a few days earlier in the street and so far unclaimed by any relative, even though all the newspapers have published her photograph.

We are all professionals, and these events are considered from a strictly professional point of view, with no wasted words, so that everything becomes quite simple, even humdrum.

'So, Maigret, haven't you arrested that Pole of yours in Rue de Birague yet?'

I hasten to declare that I have nothing against the Poles. Nor do I think, even though I may talk about them quite often, that they are an unusually violent or corrupt people. The fact, quite simply, is that at that time France, being short of workers, recruited thousands of Poles for the northern mines. In their country, whole villages were scooped up willy-nilly, men, women and children, and packed into trains, rather in the same way as black manpower was recruited at other times.

Most proved to be excellent workers, and many became respectable citizens. Nevertheless, there were dregs, as was only to be expected, and for a while those dregs gave us a hard time.

In speaking like this, in a somewhat disjointed manner, of my concerns of the moment, I am simply trying to give my reader some idea of the atmosphere.

'I'd like to have him tailed for three or four more days, chief. So far, he hasn't led us anywhere. He has to meet up with his accomplices eventually.'

'The minister's losing patience, because of the news-papers . . .'

Always the newspapers! And always, in high places, the fear of the newspapers, and of public opinion. No sooner has a crime been committed that we are enjoined to find the culprit immediately, come what may.

We would not be surprised to be told after a few days:

'Stick someone, anyone, behind bars for now, to please public opinion.'

I shall probably return to that. We did not just talk about the Pole that morning, but also about a robbery that had just been committed using a new method – a rare occur-rence.

Three days earlier, on Boulevard Saint-Denis, in the middle of the day, when most of the shops had just closed their shutters for lunch, a lorry had stopped outside a small jewel-ler's. Some men unloaded a huge crate, which they placed right up against the door, and then drove off in the lorry.

Hundreds of people passed that crate without being unduly surprised. But the jeweller, coming back from the restaurant where he had had a quick lunch, had been less sanguine.

And when he had shifted the crate, which had become very light, he had seen that an opening had been cut in the side that was against the door, another opening in the door itself, and that, of course, his shelves had been emptied, as had his safe.

It was the kind of unprestigious investigation that can demand months of work and that requires the most men. The robbers had not left a single print, or any other clue that might give them away.

The fact that the method was new made it pointless to concentrate on the usual categories of robbers.

All we had was the crate, an ordinary although very large one, and for three days a good dozen inspectors visited all the crate manufacturers, as well as all the businesses using such large crates.

Anyway, I had just got back to my office and had started writing a report when the internal telephone rang.

'Is that you, Maigret? Do you mind dropping by my office for a moment?'

Nothing surprising in that either. Almost every day, the big chief would call me at least once to his office, outside report times: I had known him since I was a child, he had often spent his holidays near us, in the Allier, and he had been a friend of my father's.

And that chief, in my eyes, really was the chief in every sense of the word, the one under whom I had started out in the Police Judiciaire, the one who, without exactly protecting me, had always kept a discreet eye on me, the one whom I had seen, dressed all in black, with a bowler hat on his head, walk alone, while bullets were flying, towards the door of the house in which Bonnot and his gang had been defying the police and the gendarmerie for two days.

I am talking about Xavier Guichard, with his mischievous eyes and long white hair like a poet's.

The daylight was so dull that morning that the lamp with the green shade was lit on his desk. Next to the desk, in an armchair, I saw a young man, who stood up and held out his hand when we were introduced.

'Inspector Maigret. Monsieur Georges Sim, a journalist—'

'Not a journalist, a novelist,' the young man protested with a smile.

Xavier Guichard also smiled. He had a range of smiles that could express all the shades of his thought. He also had at his disposal a quality of irony perceptible only to those who knew him well and which made others think of him as an innocent.

He spoke to me with the greatest seriousness, as if this was an important case, and the visitor a figure of some note.

'For his novels, Monsieur Sim needs to know how the Police Judiciaire works. As he's just been pointing out, a large proportion of human dramas end up here. He's also said that it's not so much the mechanism of the police that he'd like to have explained to him, because he's already had the opportunity to gather information elsewhere, as the atmosphere in which operations are carried out.'

I threw only brief glances at the young man, who must have been about twenty-four, thin, with hair almost as long as the chief's, and of whom the very least I can say is that he did not appear to have any doubts about anything – least of all about himself.

'Will you do him the honours of the house, Maigret?'

And, just as I was about to head for the door, I heard Sim himself say, 'I beg your pardon, Monsieur Guichard, but you forgot to tell the inspector . . .'

'Oh, yes, you're right. Monsieur Sim, as he himself has pointed out, is not a journalist. We don't run any risk that he'll reveal to the newspapers things that shouldn't be published. Without my even having to ask, he's promised that whatever he hears and sees he'll only use in his novels and in a sufficiently different form for it not to cause us any problem.'

I can still hear the chief adding gravely as he bent to look through his mail, 'You can trust him, Maigret. He's given me his word.'

Be that as it may, Xavier Guichard had let himself be bamboozled: I already sensed that, and was to have proof of it subsequently. Not only by his visitor's youth and bold-ness, but for a reason which I only discovered later. Outside his work, the chief had one passion: archaeology. He belonged to a number of learned societies, and had written a large tome (which I have never read) on the distant origins of the Paris region.

This fellow Sim knew all about that – probably not by chance – and had made a point of talking to him about it.

Was that why I was personally entrusted with the task? Almost every day, someone at the Quai is put on 'visitor duty'. Most of the time, the visitors are foreign VIPs, often with some connection or other to the police force of their country. Sometimes, they are simply influential voters from the provinces, proudly exhibiting their local deputy's business card.

It has become routine. And as with historical monuments, there is a little speech that everyone has learned more or less by heart.

But usually, an inspector will do, and a visitor has to be of major importance for the head of a department to be assigned to deal with him.

'If you like,' I suggested, 'we can go up first to the anthropometric section, where suspects are measured and photographed.'

'If it's not too much of a bother, I'd prefer to start with the waiting room.'

That was my first surprise. He said it quite gently, with a disarming look, and went on to explain:

'You see, I'd like to follow the route your customers usually follow.'

'In that case, we should start with the cells, because most of them spend the night there before being brought to us.'

To which he calmly replied, 'I visited the cells last night.'

He did not take any notes. He did not even have a notebook or pen with him. He spent several minutes in the waiting room with the glass partitions, where black-framed photographs are displayed of those members of the police who have fallen in the line of duty.

'How many die per year on average?'

Then he asked to see my office. As luck would have it, workers were busy refurbishing it at the time, and I was temporarily using an office on the mezzanine. It was an old office in the purest bureaucratic style, as dusty as you could wish for, with black wooden furniture and a coal stove of the kind you still find in some provincial railway stations.

It was the office where I had started out, where I had worked for some fifteen years as an inspector, and I admit I retained a certain fondness for that big stove. In winter, I loved to see the cast iron turn red, and I had got into the habit of filling it to the brim.

It was not so much a habit, more a front, almost a ploy. In the middle of a difficult interrogation, I would stand up and start to poke the fire for a long time, then pour in noisy shovelfuls of coal, all with a good-natured air, while the suspect would watch me, disorientated.

And it is true that, when I finally had a modern office, fitted with central heating, I missed my old stove. But I did not obtain permission to take it with me to my new location. I did not even ask for that permission, because I knew it would have been refused.

I am sorry to linger over these details, but I know more or less what I am leading up to.

My guest was looking at my pipes, my ashtrays, the black marble clock on the mantelpiece, the little enamel washstand behind the door, the towel that always smells of wet dog.

He did not ask me any technical questions. The files did not seem to interest him in the slightest.

'We can take these stairs to get to the lab.'

There too, he contemplated the partly glazed ceiling, the walls, the floors, the dummy used for reconstructions, but did not bother with the laboratory itself, its complicated apparatus, the work that was done there.

Out of habit, I tried to explain, 'By enlarging any written text hundreds of times and comparing—'

'I know. I know.'

That was when he asked me casually, 'Have you read Hans Gross?'

I had never heard the name. I subsequently discovered that he was an Austrian examining magistrate who, in about 1880, became the first professor of scientific criminology at the University of Vienna.

My visitor had read both of his two large tomes. He had read everything, all kinds of books I never even knew existed, the titles of which he would mention in a detached tone.

'Follow me into this corridor, and I'll show you the records department, where all the—'

'I know. I know.'

He was starting to get on my nerves. Anyone would have thought that the only reason he had disturbed my daily routine was in order to look at walls, ceilings and floors, and to look at all of us as if compiling a list.

'At this hour, it'll be crowded in the anthropometric section. They must have finished with the women and are starting on the men . . .'

There were about twenty of them, picked up during the night and now waiting their turn, stark naked, to be measured and photographed.

'So,' the young man said, 'all I still have left to see is the special infirmary.'

I frowned. 'Visitors aren't allowed.'

It is one of the least-known places, where criminals and suspects have to undergo a certain number of mental tests for the medical examiners.

'Paul Bourget used to attend sessions,' my visitor replied calmly. 'I'll ask for authorization.'

All told, I retained only a banal memory of it all, as banal as the weather that day. There were two reasons I did not try to cut short the visit. One was that I was doing it at the chief's request. The second was that I had nothing important to do and it managed to kill a certain amount of time.

When we got back to my office, he sat down and held out his tobacco pouch, saying, 'I see you're a pipe smoker too. I like pipe smokers.'

There were, as usual, a good half-dozen pipes on display, and he examined them like a connoisseur.

'What case are you dealing with at the moment?'

In my most professional tone, I told him about the jewel robbery, with the crate left outside, and remarked that this was the first time this method had been used.

'No,' he said. 'It was used eight years ago in New York, outside a shop on Eighth Avenue.'

He must have been pleased with himself, but I have to say he did not seem to be boasting. He smoked his pipe gravely, as if to make himself look ten years older than he was, as if to put himself on a level footing with the already mature man that I was then.

'You see, inspector, I'm not interested in professional criminals. Their psychology is quite straightforward. They're simply doing their job, that's all.'

'What *are* you interested in?'

'The others. Those who are just like you and me, and who end up committing a murder one fine day without having planned it.'

'There are very few.'

'I know.'

'Apart from crimes of passion.'

'Crimes of passion don't interest me either.'

That is more or less everything I recall of that encounter. I must have told him in passing about a case that had required my attention some months earlier, precisely because it did not concern professionals, a case involving a young girl and a pearl necklace.

'I'm very grateful, inspector. I hope I'll have the pleasure of meeting you again.'

To myself, I said, 'I hope not.'

Weeks passed, then months. Only once, in the middle of winter, did I have the impression I saw the man named Sim, pacing up and down in the main corridor of the Police Judiciaire.

One morning, I found on my desk, beside my mail, a small book, printed on bad paper, with a horrible illustration on the cover, the kind you see on news vendor's stands and in the hands of shop girls. The title was *The Girl with the Pearl Necklace*, and the name of the author was Georges Sim.

I was not curious enough to read it. I do not read much, and never that kind of pulp novel. I do not even know where I put the book, probably in the waste-paper basket, and for some days I thought no more about it.

Then, another morning, I found an identical book in the same place on my desk, and now, every morning, a new copy made its appearance next to my mail.

It took me a while to realize that my inspectors, particularly Lucas, were sometimes glancing at me in an amused way. At last, one lunchtime when we went and had an aperitif together at the Brasserie Dauphine, Lucas, after beating about the bush for a long time, said:

'So now you've become a fictional character, chief.'

He took the book from his pocket.

'Have you read it?'

He admitted that it was Janvier, the youngest in the squad at the time, who had been putting a copy of the book on my desk every morning.

'In some ways it's quite like you, you'll see.'

He was right. It was like me in the same way that a drawing scribbled on a marble-topped café table by an amateur cartoonist is like an actual flesh and blood person.

In the book, I was bigger than in real life, heavier too, with a heaviness that was, if I can put it this way, positively ponderous.

As for the story, it was unrecognizable, and in the plot I used methods that were unexpected to say the least.

The same evening, I found my wife with the book in her hands.

'It was the dairy maid who gave it to me. Apparently they're all talking about you. I haven't had time to read it yet.'

What could I do? As the man named Sim promised, it was not a newspaper. Nor was it a serious book, but a cheap publication to which it would have been absurd to attach any importance.

He had used my real name. But he could have retorted that there are a certain number of Maigrets in the world. I simply vowed to receive him quite coldly if by any chance I met him again, although I was convinced that he would avoid setting foot in the Police Judiciaire from now on.

But I was wrong about that. One day, when I knocked at the chief's door without having been summoned, in order to ask for his opinion about something, he called out:

'Come in, Maigret. I was just about to phone you. Our friend Sim is here.'

Our friend Sim was not embarrassed at all. On the contrary, he was absolutely at his ease, with a bigger pipe than ever in his mouth.

'How are you, inspector?'

'He's just read me a few passages from the thing he's written about the house,' Guichard said.

'I already know it.'

Guichard had an amused gleam in his eyes, but it was me he seemed to be making fun of this time.

'He's been making some very relevant points. I think you should hear them. He'll tell you himself.'

'It's quite simple. In France up until now, with very rare exceptions, the sympathetic role in literature has always been played by the criminal, while the police are ridiculed, or worse.'

Guichard was nodding approvingly. 'That's true, isn't it?'

It was indeed true. Not only in literature, but also in everyday life. That brought back a somewhat bitter memory from my early days, at a time when I was on the beat. I was just about to arrest a pickpocket outside a Métro station when the man started yelling something – 'Stop, thief!' perhaps.

Instantly, twenty people jumped on me. I told them that I was a policeman, and that the individual walking away was a repeat offender. I am convinced they all believed me. And yet they did everything they could to delay me, thus giving the pickpocket time to get away.

'Well,' Guichard went on, 'our friend Sim is planning to write a series of novels in which the police will be shown in their true light.'

I made a grimace that did not escape the chief.

'More or less in their true light,' he corrected himself. 'Do you understand? This book is only a sketch of what he plans to do.'

'He used my name in it.'

I thought the young man would be embarrassed and apologize. Not at all.

'I hope you weren't shocked by that. I couldn't help myself. When I imagine a character with a particular name, I find it impossible to change it. I tried in vain to put together all the syllables you could possibly think of to replace the word Maigret. In the end, I gave up. He wouldn't have been *my* character any more.'

He said *my* character, calmly, and the worst of it was that I did not react, perhaps because of Guichard and the mischievous gaze he kept fixed on me.

'This time, it wouldn't be a series of pulp novels, but what he calls . . . How was it you put it, Monsieur Sim?'

'Semi-literature.'

'And you want me to . . .'

'I'd like to get to know you better.'

As I said when I started: he had no doubts. I even think it was his strength. It was partly thanks to this that he had already managed to get the chief on his side.

Guichard, who was interested in all specimens of humanity, now said to me quite gravely, 'He's only twenty-four.'

'I find it hard to construct a character if I don't know how he acts at every moment of the day. For example, I can't write about a millionaire until I've actually seen one in his dressing gown, having a boiled egg for breakfast.'

All this happened a long time ago, and I wonder now for what mysterious reason we listened to all this without bursting out laughing.

'So, you'd like . . .'

'To get to know you better, to see you living and working.'

Of course, the chief did not give me any orders. I would doubtless have objected. For some time now, I had been wondering if this was all a hoax on his part. He still had a certain bohemian side to his character, from the days when bohemians went in for practical jokes.

It was probably to give the impression that I did not take any of this too seriously that I shrugged and said, 'Whenever you like.'

At which Sim stood up, delighted. 'Straight away.'

Once again, with hindsight, it may seem ridiculous. The dollar was worth some improbable amount. The Americans lit their cigars with thousand-franc notes. Montmartre was filled with Negro musicians, and wealthy mature ladies had their jewellery stolen at tea dances by Argentinian gigolos.

La Garçonne was a huge bestseller, and the vice squad were up to their eyes in 'orgies' in the Bois de Boulogne which they hardly dared interrupt for fear of catching consular officials in the act.

Women wore their hair short, their skirts too, and men wore pointed shoes and trousers tapered at the ankles.

That is no explanation for anything, I know. But everything is part of everything. And I can still see young Sim coming into my office in the morning, as if he had become one of my inspectors, saying pleasantly, 'Don't put yourself out,' and sitting down in a corner.

He still did not take any notes. He asked few questions. He preferred statements to questions. He told me subsequently – not that I necessarily believed him – that someone's reaction to a statement is more revealing than his answer to a specific question.

One lunchtime, when Lucas, Janvier and I went to have our aperitif at the Brasserie Dauphine, as we often did, he joined us.

And one morning, when I went to the chief's office for the daily report, I found him sitting in a corner of the room.

This lasted a few months. When I asked him what he was writing, he replied:

'I'm still turning out pulp novels to earn my living. From four to eight in the morning. By eight o'clock I've finished my day. I'll only start on my semi-literary novels when I feel ready.'

I have no idea what he meant by that, but, after a Sunday when I invited him to lunch in my apartment on Boulevard Richard-Lenoir and introduced him to my wife, he suddenly stopped his visits to Quai des Orfèvres.

It was an odd feeling to no longer see him in his corner, standing up when I stood up, following me when I left and accompanying me step by step through the offices.

Sometime in the spring, I received a card that was unexpected to say the least.

> Georges Sim has the honour to invite you to the christening of his boat, the *Ostrogoth*, as performed by the Curé of Notre-Dame, next Tuesday, at Square du Vert-Galant.

I did not go. I heard later from the local police that for three days and three nights a gang of bizarre characters had made a great racket on board a sumptuously appointed boat moored bang in the middle of Paris.

Once, crossing the Pont-Neuf, I saw the boat in question, and at the foot of the mast, someone typing, wearing a sea captain's cap.

The following week, the boat was no longer there and Square du Vert-Galant had returned to normal.

More than a year later, I received another invitation, written this time on one of our fingerprint charts.

Georges Simenon has the honour of inviting you to the anthropometric ball which will be held at the *Boule Blanche* on the occasion of the launch of his detective novels.

Sim had become Simenon.

Or to be more precise, feeling perhaps that he was now an adult, he had gone back to his real name.

I took no notice. I did not attend the ball in question, although I found out the following day that the prefect of police had gone.

Through the newspapers. The same newspapers that informed me, on the front page, that Chief Inspector Maigret had just made a striking entrance into the field of detective fiction.

That morning, when I arrived at the Quai and climbed the main staircase, I saw only sardonic smiles, amused faces turning away.

My inspectors were doing everything they could to keep a straight face. During the daily report, my colleagues pretended to treat me with new respect.

It was only the chief who behaved as if nothing had happened, and who asked me, with an absent air, 'What about you, Maigret? What about your current cases?'

In the shops in the Richard-Lenoir area, not a single shopkeeper neglected to show my wife the newspaper, with my name in capital letters, and ask her, impressed, 'This is your husband, isn't it?'

Unfortunately, it was!

2.

In which there is some discussion of what is called the naked truth, which convinces nobody, and of 'organized' truths which are truer than life

When it became known that I was writing this book, and then that Simenon's publisher had offered to publish it, even before reading it, even before the first chapter was finished, I sensed, among most of my friends, a somewhat hesitant approval. I am sure they were saying to themselves, 'Now it's Maigret's turn!'

Over the course of the last few years, as it happens, at least three of my former colleagues, from those of my generation, have written and published their memoirs.

I hasten to add that in this they have followed an old tradition of the Paris police, which has given us, among other things, the memoirs of Macé and those of the great Goron, both chiefs in their day of what was then called the Sûreté. As for the most famous of all, the legendary Vidocq, he unfortunately did not leave us any recollections of his own that we can compare with the way he has been depicted by novelists, who have called him by his real name, or, as in the case of Balzac, Vautrin.

It is not my role to defend my colleagues, but I can nevertheless reply in passing to an objection I have often heard.

'To judge by what they wrote,' people have said to me, 'every famous case has been solved by at least three people.'

The case that was particularly cited was the Mestorino case, which once caused a great stir.

Well, I could include myself too, because a case of that significance requires the collaboration of all the departments. As for the final interrogation, that famous twenty-eight-hour interrogation that is cited today as an example, there were not just four, but at least six of us who took turns, repeating the same questions one by one, in every conceivable way, each time gaining a little more ground.

In such circumstances, anybody who could say for certain which of us, at a given moment, triggered the final confession, would be clever indeed.

Besides, I insist on declaring that the title *Memoirs* was not chosen by me, and has been given to the book only as a last resort, after we failed to find another word.

The same is true (I underline this as I correct the proofs) of the chapter headings, which the publisher has asked my permission to add after the event, for typographical reasons, as he kindly put it – in reality, I think, to give my text a touch of humour.

Of all the tasks I did at Quai des Orfèvres, the only one about which I never complained was the writing of reports. Is that because of an atavistic concern for accuracy, a scrupulousness I saw my father struggle with before me?

I have often heard the almost classic quip: 'Maigret's reports are full of parentheses.'

Probably because I want to explain too much, to explain everything, because nothing seems simple or resolved.

If, by 'memoirs', people mean an account of events in which I have been involved in the course of my career, I fear the public will be disappointed.

In the space of nearly half a century, I do not think there were more than twenty or so really sensational cases, including those to which I have already referred – the Bonnot case, the Mestorino case – plus the Landru case, the Sarret case and a few others.

But my colleagues, my former chiefs in some cases, have written a great deal about those.

As for the other cases, those that were interesting in themselves but caused no stir in the newspapers, Simenon has taken care of them.

At last I have come to what I have been leading up to, or trying to lead up to, ever since I began this manuscript – in other words, the real reason I am writing these memoirs that are not memoirs – and I am even less sure now than I was then as to how to express myself.

I read once in the newspapers that Anatole France, who must have been an intelligent man at the very least and who loved irony, having posed for a portrait by the painter

Van Dongen, not only refused to take delivery of it once the painting was finished, but forbade it from being exhibited in public.

It was around the same time that a famous actress brought a sensational case against a cartoonist who had depicted her in a way that she considered outrageous and damaging to her career.

I am neither an Academician nor a stage star. I do not think I am unusually sensitive. Never, in all the years I have exercised my profession, have I ever demanded an apology from the press, even though the newspapers have had no qualms in criticizing my actions or my methods.

It is no longer given to everyone to commission a portrait from a painter, but these days everyone has at least had the experience of being photographed. And I suppose everyone knows that sense of discomfort that seizes us when faced with an image of ourselves that is not quite right.

I hope what I am trying to say is understood. I feel somewhat ashamed to insist. I know I am touching on an essential, highly sensitive point and, unusually for me, I suddenly feel afraid of ridicule.

I think it would be more or less of no consequence to me if I were depicted in ways that are completely different from the way I really am, even to the point of verging on slander.

But I come back to the analogy of photography. The lens does not allow complete inaccuracy. The image is different without really being different. Faced with a photograph, you are sometimes incapable of putting your finger on the detail that shocks you, of saying exactly *what* is not you, *what* you do not recognize as yourself.

Well, for years, such was my situation in relation to Simenon's Maigret, whom I could see growing every day by my side, to the point that people were eventually asking me in good faith if I had copied his mannerisms, others if my name was really my father's name or if I had borrowed it from Simenon.

I have tried to explain as best I could how things happened at the beginning: innocently, without any sense that it might have consequences.

The very fact that the fellow to whom good old Xavier Guichard introduced me in his office one day was so young gave me no cause for suspicion, but rather made me somewhat dismissive.

But a few months later, I was well and truly caught in a mechanism from which I have never emerged, and the pages I am writing now will not save me from it entirely.

'What are you complaining about? You're famous!'

I know! I know! People say that when they have not been through it. I even concede that there are times, and certain circumstances, when it is not unpleasant. Not just because it boosts my self-esteem, but often for practical reasons: being able to get a good seat in a train or a crowded restaurant, not having to queue for things.

For many years, I did not object, any more than I demanded apologies from the newspapers.

Nor am I suddenly claiming that I was seething inside, or champing at the bit. That would be an exaggeration, and I hate exaggeration.

But I did promise myself that one day I would say what I have to say, with good humour and without any resentment, and that I would make things clear once and for all.

And that day has arrived.

Why is this book called *Memoirs*? I am not responsible for that, I repeat, and the word was not chosen by me.

I am not going to talk about Mestorino, or Landru, or the lawyer in the Massif Central who killed his victims by plunging them in a bath tub filled with quicklime.

No, what I am doing is simply confronting a character with a character, a truth with a truth.

I will explain immediately what some people mean by truth.

It was right at the beginning, at the time of that anthropometric ball which, along with some other more or less spectacular and tasteful manifestations, launched what were already being called the first Maigrets, two books entitled *The Hanged Man of Saint-Pholien* and *The Late Monsieur Gallet*.

I shall not conceal the fact that I read both books immediately. And I can still see Simenon coming into my office the next day, pleased with himself, displaying even more self-confidence, if possible, than before, but nevertheless with a touch of anxiety in his eyes.

'I know what you're going to say!' he cried even before I could open my mouth.

He began pacing up and down.

'I know the books are filled with technical errors,' he went on. 'There's no point counting them. They're quite deliberate, and I'll tell you why.'

I did not register everything he said, but I remember the essential phrase, which he often repeated to me subsequently, with a satisfaction verging on sadism:

'The truth never seems true. I don't just mean in literature or painting. Do I even need to mention Doric columns? We think they're absolutely straight, but they only give that impression because they're slightly bent. If they were straight, our eyes would see them as bulging outwards.'

In those days, he still liked to show off his erudition.

'Tell anyone a story. If you don't organize it, it'll be considered incredible, artificial. Organize it, and it'll seem truer than life.'

He trumpeted these last words as if they were a sensational discovery.

'Making it seem truer than life, that's the crux of it. Well, I've made you truer than life.'

I was speechless. In the heat of the moment, the poor chief inspector that I was, the chief inspector who was 'less true than life', could find nothing to say in reply.

And with an abundance of gestures and a hint of a Belgian accent, he went on to demonstrate to me that my investigations, as he had told them, were more plausible – did he actually say 'more accurate'? – than the way I had experienced them.

During our first encounters in the autumn, he had not been lacking in self-confidence. Now, thanks to his success, he was brimming over with it, he had enough to give away to all the timorous people in the world.

'Let me explain . . . In a real investigation, there are sometimes fifty officers, maybe even more, involved in searching for the culprit. It's not just you and your inspectors following leads. The police and the gendarmerie throughout the country are alerted. A watch is kept on the stations, in the ports, at the borders. Not to mention the informers, let alone the amateurs who join in the game.

'Try, in the two hundred or two hundred and fifty pages of a novel, to give a more or less faithful account of all that activity! A multi-volume saga wouldn't be enough, and after a few chapters, the reader would get totally confused and be put off.

'But in real life, who is there every morning to stop things getting confused, who is there to put everyone in their places and concentrate on the crucial lead?'

He looked me up and down triumphantly.

'It's you, as you know perfectly well. It's the person leading the investigation. I'm well aware that a chief inspector in the Police Judiciaire, the head of a special squad, doesn't run around the streets in person questioning concierges and bar owners.

'And I'm also aware that, except in exceptional cases, you don't spend your nights pacing deserted streets in the rain, waiting for a light to come on in a window, or a door to open.

'All the same, it's exactly as if you were there yourself, aren't I right?'

What could I say to that? From a certain point of view, it was logical.

'Simplification! The first quality, the essential quality of a truth is to be simple. And I've simplified. I've reduced the machinery around you to its simplest expression, but the result hasn't changed anything at all.

'Instead of fifty more or less anonymous inspectors running around in confusion, I've kept just three or four, each with his own personality.'

'The others aren't happy,' I tried to object.

'I'm not writing for a few dozen officers in the Police Judiciaire. If you write a book about teachers, whatever you do you're bound to upset tens of thousands of teachers. It'd be the same if you wrote about stationmasters or typists. Where were we?'

'The different kinds of truths.'

'I was trying to demonstrate to you that mine is the only valid one. Would you like another example? There's no need to have spent the days I've spent in this building to know that the Police Judiciaire, being part of the Prefecture of Police, can only operate within the boundaries of Paris, and by extension, in some cases, in the Department of the Seine.

'But in *The Late Monsieur Gallet* I write about an investigation that took place in the centre of France.

'Have you been there, yes or no?'

Of course, I had.

'It's true, I have been there, but at a time when—'

'At a time when, for a while, you worked, not for the Police Judiciaire, but for the Sûreté. Why bother the reader with these bureaucratic niceties?

'Should I explain at the beginning of each book: "This happened in such and such a year, when Maigret was attached to such and such a department"?

'Let me finish . . .'

He knew he was about to touch on a sensitive subject, but would not let go.

'In your habits, in your attitudes, in your character, where do you most belong? Are you a man of Quai des Orfèvres, or a man of Rue des Saussaies?'

I beg pardon of my colleagues in the Sûreté, among whom I have some good friends, but I am not telling anyone anything new in admitting that there is, let us say, at the very least a rivalry between the two houses, the Police Judiciaire on Quai des Orfèvres and the Sûreté in Rue des Saussaies.

Let us also admit something that Simenon had grasped from the start, which is that at that time in particular there were two quite different types of police officer.

The men of Rue des Saussaies, who report directly to the Minister of the Interior, find themselves, by the force of things, handling political matters.

I do not hold it against them. I simply confess that, as far as I am concerned, I prefer not to have to deal with such things.

Our field of activity at Quai des Orfèvres may be more restrictive, more down to earth. We are concerned with villains of all kinds, with everything that comes within the concept of a criminal investigation department.

'You'll concede that you're a man of the Quai. You're proud of it. Well, I've made you a man of the Quai. I've tried to make you the embodiment of it. Should I, for the sake of accuracy, because I know you're obsessed with accuracy, confuse that image by pointing out that in a particular year, for complicated reasons, you temporarily switched to the other house, which allowed you to work in the four corners of France?'

'But—'

'One moment. The first day I met you, I told you I wasn't a journalist, but a novelist, and I remember promising Monsieur Guichard that my books would never contain any indiscretions that might cause his department problems.'

'I know, but—'

'Wait, Maigret, for heaven's sake!'

It was the first time he had called me that. It was also the first time this young man had shut me up.

'I've changed the names, except for yours and those of two or three of your colleagues. I've also taken care to change the locations. Often I've even taken the precaution of changing the characters' family relationships.

'I've simplified. Sometimes I've left only one interrogation, where you must have carried out four or five, only two or three avenues of inquiry where you may at first have been faced with ten of them.

'I claim that I'm the one who's right, that my truth is the right one. I've brought you proof.'

He pointed to a pile of books he had placed on my desk when he arrived and to which I had not paid any attention.

'These are the books written by specialists in police matters over the last twenty years, true stories, the kind of truth you like.

'Read them. You know most of the cases these books talk about in detail.

'Well, I bet you won't recognize them, precisely because the concern for objectivity falsifies the truth, which is always, which must always be simple.

'And now . . .'

At this point, I'd like to get straight down to my confession. It was at that precise moment that I realized what was really bothering me.

He was right, for heaven's sake, on all the points he had just enumerated. It hardly mattered to me, any more than it did to him, that he had reduced the number of inspectors, or that he had me spending my nights in the rain instead of them, or that, deliberately or not, he had mixed up the Sûreté with the Police Judiciaire.

The thing that shocked me, when it came down to it, the thing I did not yet want to admit to myself, was . . .

My God, how difficult this is! Remember what I said about the man looking at his photograph.

Let us take just the question of the bowler hat. Too bad if I look ridiculous when I confess that this stupid detail caused me more upset than all the others.

When young Sim came to Quai des Orfèvres for the first time, I still had a bowler hat in my wardrobe, but I only wore it on rare occasions: for funerals or official ceremonies.

Now it so happens that a photograph was hanging in my office, taken some years earlier during some conference or other, in which I was shown wearing that damned hat.

As a consequence of which I still hear, when I am introduced to people who have never seen me:

'Oh, you've changed your hat!'

As for the famous overcoat with the velvet collar, it was not to me but to my wife that Simenon was eventually to furnish an explanation.

I did have one, I admit. I even had several, like all men of my generation. I may well have taken down one of those old coats on a cold rainy day in or around 1927.

I am no dandy. I do not care much for elegance. But perhaps because of that, I hate standing out. And my little Jewish tailor in Rue de Turenne is no more desirous than I am of people turning to look at me in the street.

'Is it my fault I see you like that?' Simenon could have replied, like a painter giving his sitter a lopsided nose or a squint.

Only the sitter in question is not forced to spend his whole life face to face with his portrait, and there are not thousands of people believing for ever more that he has a lopsided nose or a squint.

I did not say all this to him that morning. Modestly, I made do with looking away and saying, 'Did you really have to simplify me too?'

'At first, yes. The public has to get used to you, to your outline, your walk. I think I've just found the word. For the moment, you're still nothing but an outline, a back, a pipe, a way of walking, of grunting.'

'Thank you.'

'The details will appear little by little, you'll see. I don't know how long it'll take, but gradually you'll become subtler, more complex, more alive.'

'That's reassuring.'

'For example, you don't yet have a home life, even though Boulevard Richard-Lenoir and Madame Maigret constitute at least half of your existence. All you've done so far is phone home, but we'll see you there.'

'In my dressing gown and slippers?'

'Even in bed.'

'I wear nightshirts,' I said ironically.

'I know. That's the perfect touch. Even if you'd switched to pyjamas, I'd have given you a nightshirt.'

I wonder how this conversation would have finished – probably with an argument – if I had not been told that a petty informer from Rue Pigalle was asking to speak to me.

'So all in all,' I said to Simenon as he held out his hand, 'you're pleased with yourself.'

'Not yet, but it'll come.'

Could I have told him that I forbade him to use my name from now on? Legally, yes. And that would have given rise to what is known as a very Parisian trial, which would only have made me look ridiculous.

The character would have been called something else. But he would still have been me, or more precisely that simplified version of me, which, if his author was to be believed, would gradually become more complex.

The worst of it was that the fellow was not mistaken and that each month, for years, I would open a book with a photographic cover and find a Maigret who was more and more like me.

If only he had stayed in books! But the cinema would soon join in, and later the radio and the television.

It is a strange feeling to see up there on the screen, coming and going, talking, wiping his nose, a man who claims to be you, who has a number of your mannerisms, says things you have said, in situations you have experienced, sometimes in settings which have been meticulously reconstructed.

With the first screen Maigret, Pierre Renoir, the result was more or less convincing. I was made a little taller, a little thinner. The face, of course, was different, but some bits of behaviour were so striking that I suspect the actor may have observed me without my noticing.

A few months later, I was twenty centimetres shorter, and what I lost in height I gained in girth, becoming, as played by Abel Tarride, a fat, easy-going fellow, so soft that I looked like a balloon animal about to fly up to the ceiling. Not to mention the knowing winks with which I underlined how clever I was!

I did not stay to the end of the film, and my troubles were not over.

Harry Baur was doubtless a great actor, but he was a good twenty years older than me at the time, with a face that was both soft and tragic.

Let us move on!

Much later, having previously aged twenty years, I grew almost twenty years younger, in the shape of an actor named Préjean, whom I do not blame in the slightest – any more than I blame the others – but who looked much more like some young inspectors today than those of my generation.

Last but not least, I have recently been inflated again, inflated to the point of exploding, and simultaneously, in the guise of Charles Laughton, made to speak English as if it were my mother tongue.

Well, of all of them, there was at least one who had the good taste to go behind Simenon's back and discover that my truth was better than his.

It was Pierre Renoir, who did not have a bowler hat on his head, but wore a quite ordinary soft hat and clothes such as any public official would wear, whether or not he was in the police.

I realize I have spoken only of unimportant details, a hat, a coat, a coal stove, probably because it is those details that shocked me first.

We are not surprised when we grow up and then become old. But a man simply has to cut off the ends of his moustache and he will cease to recognize himself.

To be honest, I prefer to deal with what I consider small weaknesses, before comparing the two characters in depth.

If Simenon is right, which is quite possible, mine will start to seem colourless and insubstantial beside his famous simplified – or organized – truth, and I will look like a bad-tempered man re-touching his own portrait.

Now that I have started, with clothes, I have to continue, if only for my own peace of mind.

Simenon asked me recently – by the way, he too has changed from the young man I encountered in Xavier Guichard's office – Simenon asked me, in a somewhat mocking tone:

'Well? How's the new Maigret coming along?'

I tried to reply with the words he had once used.

'He's taking shape! He's still just an outline. A hat. A coat. But it's his real hat. His real coat! Maybe the rest will come gradually, and he'll have two arms, two legs, maybe even a face? Maybe he'll start to think for himself, without the help of a novelist.'

By the way, Simenon is now more or less the same age I was when we first met. At that time, he had a tendency to consider me as a mature, or even old, man.

I did not ask him what he thought about that today, but I could not help remarking:

'Do you know, with the years you've started walking, smoking a pipe, even talking like *your* Maigret?'

Which is true, and which gives me – I hope the reader will grant me that – a quite delicious feeling of revenge.

It is rather as if, late in the day, he was starting to think *he* was *me*!

3.

In which I will try to speak about a bearded doctor who influenced the life of my family and perhaps, when it comes down to it, my choice of career

I do not know if I will find the right tone this time. This morning, I have already filled my waste-paper basket with torn-up pages.

And last night I was on the point of giving up. As my wife read what I had written during the day, I watched her while pretending to read the newspaper, as usual. After a while, I had the impression something had startled her, and from then until the end, she kept throwing me surprised, almost pained little glances.

Instead of speaking to me immediately, she walked silently to the drawer and put the manuscript away. It was a while before she said, making an effort to keep her comment as light as possible:

'It sounds as if you don't like him.'

There was no need to ask her who she meant, and now it was my turn not to understand, to look at her wide-eyed.

'What are you talking about?' I exclaimed. 'Since when has Simenon stopped being our friend?'

'Yes, obviously . . .'

Trying to recall what I had written, I wondered what it was she might have at the back of her mind.

'I might be wrong,' she said. 'I must be wrong, since you say so. But I had the impression, reading some passages, that you were expressing a genuine resentment. Please don't get me wrong. Not the big kind of resentment we admit to. Something more muted, more . . .'

She didn't add the word – I did it for her: ' . . . More shameful . . .'

I can honestly say that, in writing, that was far from my intention. Not only had I always had the most cordial relations with Simenon, but he had soon become a family friend, and the few times we went away in the summer it was almost always to visit him in his successive residences when he was still living in France: in Alsace, on Porquerolles, in the Charente, in the Vendée, and Lord knows where else. More recently, when I agreed to go on a semi-official tour of the United States, it may have been because I knew I could see him in Arizona, where he was then living.

'I swear to you . . .' I began gravely.

'I believe you. It's the readers who may not.'

It is my fault, I am convinced of it. I am not very good at irony, and I realize that when I attempt it, it must seem quite heavy. Out of a kind of modesty, I have actually been trying to handle a difficult subject, one that is somewhat wounding to my pride, in a fairly light-hearted manner.

In short, what I have been trying to do is nothing more, nothing less than to adjust one image to another image, a character, not to its shadow, but to its double. And Simenon was the very first to encourage me in this undertaking.

To soothe my wife, who is almost fiercely loyal in her friendships, I hasten to say that Simenon, as I said yesterday in other terms, because I was joking, is nothing like the young man whose aggressive self-confidence sometimes made me raise an eyebrow. On the contrary, it is he who has now grown deliberately taciturn and speaks with a certain hesitation, especially about the subjects closest to his heart, fearing to make assertions, looking – I would swear – for my approval.

Having said that, will I tease him again? A little bit, in spite of everything. It will probably be the last time. The opportunity is too good to miss.

In the forty or so books he has devoted to my investigations, there may well be only about twenty references to my background or my family: a few words about my father and his profession as an estate manager, a mention of the school in Nantes where I studied for a while, some very brief allusions to my two years as a medical student.

This, of course, is the same man who needed nearly eight hundred pages to recount his childhood up until the age of sixteen. Little matter that he did it in the form of a novel, or whether his characters were accurate or not, he seemed to believe that his hero was only complete when surrounded by his parents and grandparents, his uncles and his aunts, whose every fault, illness, little vice and tumour he reports to us. Even his neighbour's dog gets half a page.

I am not complaining. The only reason I am pointing this out is that it is an indirect way of defending myself in advance from the accusation that might be made that I am spending too much time talking about my family.

As far as I am concerned, a man without a past is not completely a man. In the course of certain investigations, I have sometimes paid more attention to a suspect's family and entourage than to the suspect himself, and it is often in this way that I have discovered the key to what might otherwise have remained a mystery.

It has been said, correctly, that I was born in the centre of France, not far from Moulins, but I do not recall it having been made clear that the estate of which my father was the manager was a property of three thousand hectares, on which there were no fewer than twenty-six smallholdings.

Not only was my grandfather, whom I knew, one of the tenant farmers who worked these smallholdings, but he was the descendant of at least three generations of Maigrets who had tilled the same land.

When my father was young, a typhus epidemic decimated the family, which included seven or eight children, leaving only two survivors, my father and one sister, who would later marry a baker and move to Nantes.

Why did my father go to the secondary school in Moulins, thus breaking with such long-established traditions? I have every reason to believe that the village priest took an interest in him. But it was not a complete break with the land, because, after two years in a school of agriculture, he came back to the village and went into service at the chateau as assistant estate manager.

I still feel a certain embarrassment talking about him. I have the impression, in fact, that people say to each other:

'The image he's kept of his parents is the kind of image we have of our parents when we're children.'

And for a long time, I wondered if I was mistaken, if my critical spirit might have been at fault.

But I have sometimes met other men like him, especially among those of his generation, most of them in the same social position, a position that might be called intermediate.

For my grandfather, the people in the chateau – their rights, their privileges, their behaviour – were not up for discussion. What he thought about them deep down, I never knew. I was still young when he died. I nevertheless remain convinced, remembering certain looks, and, in particular, certain silences, that his approval was not passive, that it was not even always approval, or resignation, but that it derived, on the contrary, from a certain pride, and above all from a very strong sense of duty.

It was that feeling that endured in men like my father, combined with a reserve, a need for decency that might have seemed like resignation.

I can still picture him very well. I have kept photographs of him. He was very tall, very thin, and his thinness was exaggerated by narrow trousers covered until just below the knee by leather gaiters. I always saw my father in leather gaiters. It was a kind of uniform for him. He did not have a beard, but long reddish-blond whiskers in which, when he came home in winter, I felt little ice crystals as I kissed him.

Our house was in the courtyard of the chateau, a pretty two-storey pink brick house, which stood out from the low buildings where the families of valets, grooms and guards lived, men whose wives mostly worked in the chateau as laundresses, dressmakers or kitchen maids.

In that courtyard, my father was a kind of monarch, to whom the men spoke with respect, doffing their caps.

About once a week, soon after nightfall, sometimes as early as dusk, he would set off in his cart with one or more tenant farmers for some distant fair, to buy or sell animals. He would not return until the following evening.

His office was in a separate building. On the walls were photographs of prize bulls and horses, calendars of fairs and, almost always, drying as the year went on, the finest sheaf of corn gathered on the estate.

At about ten o'clock, he would cross the courtyard and enter a world apart. Walking around the outside of the buildings, he would climb the large front steps, beyond which the farmers never went, and spend a certain time within the thick walls of the chateau.

In a way, it was an equivalent for him of what the morning report is for us in the Police Judiciaire, and, as a child, I was proud to see him climbing that prestigious flight of steps, looking very erect and without a trace of servility.

He spoke little, and rarely laughed, but when he did you were surprised to discover how young, almost childish, his laughter was, and to see him amused by quite silly jokes.

He did not drink, unlike most of the people I knew. At each meal, a little carafe reserved for him would be put on the table, half filled with a light white wine harvested on the estate, and I never saw him have anything else, even at weddings and funerals. And at fairs, where he was obliged to frequent the inns, he was automatically brought a cup of coffee, to which he was partial.

In my eyes, he was a man, and more specifically a man of a certain age. I was five years old when my grandfather died. As for my maternal grandparents, they lived more than fifty kilometres away, and we only visited them twice a year so that I did not really know them. They were not farmers. They owned a grocery in quite a large town, with a bar attached to it, as is often the case in the country.

I could not say for sure today, but that may well have been the reason our relations with the in-laws were not closer.

I was just under eight when I finally noticed that my mother was pregnant. Through whispers and words caught by chance, I more or less grasped that the pregnancy was unexpected, that after my birth the doctors had decreed that any more children were unlikely.

I reconstructed most of this later, piece by piece, which I suppose is always the way with childhood memories.

At that time, in the next village, which was larger than ours, there was a doctor with a pointed red beard named

Gadelle – Victor Gadelle, if I am not mistaken – of whom people did not speak much, and almost always with an air of mystery. It may have been because of his beard, and also because of everything that was said about him, but I think I almost thought of him as some kind of devil.

There was a tragedy in his life, a real tragedy, the first I had ever heard about and one that made a great impression on me, especially as it was to have a profound influence on our family, and through that, on my entire life.

Gadelle drank. He drank more than any of the local farmers, not only from time to time, but every day, starting in the morning and only finishing at night. He drank enough to spread a smell of alcohol through a warm room, a smell that always filled me with disgust.

In addition, he did not take much care of his appearance. It might even be said that he was dirty.

How, in such circumstances, could he be my father's friend? That was a mystery to me. But the fact is that he often came to our house and chatted with him, and there was even a ritual: as soon as he arrived, a decanter of brandy which was reserved only for him was taken from the windowed dresser.

Of the first tragedy, I knew almost nothing at the time. Dr Gadelle's wife had fallen pregnant, for what must have been for the sixth or seventh time. To me, she was already an old woman, although she was probably only about forty.

What happened the day she went into labour? Apparently, Gadelle got home even drunker than usual, and as he sat by his wife's bedside, waiting for the delivery, he continued to drink.

The wait was longer than normal. The children had been taken to the neighbours. Towards morning, as nothing was happening, the sister-in-law, who had spent the night in the house, had left to check how things were in her own home.

It seems there were screams, a lot of commotion, a lot of movement in the doctor's house.

When they went in, Gadelle was weeping in a corner. His wife was dead. So was the child.

And, for a long time afterwards, I would still catch the local gossips whispering in each other's ears, with indignant or dismayed expressions:

'A real bloodbath!'

For months the Gadelle case was the subject of all conversations. As was only to be expected, it divided the area into two camps.

Some – and there were many of them – went to the town, which was then a real journey, to see another doctor, while others, indifferent or still trusting in spite of it all, continued to call Gadelle.

My father never confided in me about the subject. I am therefore reduced to speculating.

What I know for certain is that Gadelle never stopped coming to see us. He would come in just as in the past, in the course of his rounds, and the routine was still observed of placing the famous decanter with the gilded edge in front of him.

He drank less, though. It was said that he was no longer seen drunk. One night, in the most distant of the smallholdings, he was called out to a labour and acquitted himself honourably. On his way home, he dropped into our house, but I remember that he was very pale. I can see my father shaking his hand with an insistence that was not in his nature, as if to encourage him, as if to tell him, 'You see, it wasn't hopeless.'

Because my father never despaired of people. I never heard him utter an irrevocable judgement, even when the black sheep of the estate, a loud-mouthed tenant farmer whose embezzling he must have reported to the chateau, accused him of some dishonest scheme or other.

In the case of Gadelle, if there had been nobody to hold out his hand to him after the death of his wife and child, he would have been lost.

My father did that. And when my mother was pregnant, a feeling I find hard to explain, but which I can understand, made him persevere.

Nevertheless, he took precautions. Twice in the later stages of her pregnancy, he took my mother to Moulins to see a specialist.

The time came. A stable boy rode out to fetch the doctor some time in the middle of the night. I was not made to leave the house, but remained shut in my room, terribly upset, even though, like all country children, I had a certain knowledge of these things even when I was young.

My mother died at seven in the morning, as day was breaking, and when I went downstairs the first object that attracted my attention, in spite of my emotion, was the decanter on the dining-room table.

I remained an only child. A local girl moved into the house to do the chores and take care of me. I never saw Dr Gadelle cross our threshold after that, nor did I ever hear my father say a word about him.

A very grey, confused period followed this tragedy. I was going to the village school. My father spoke less and less. He was thirty-two years old, and it is only now that I realize how young he was.

I made no objection when I turned twelve and it was decided to send me to the secondary school in Moulins – as a boarder, because it was impossible to take me there every day.

I only spent a few months there. I was unhappy, a complete stranger in a new world that seemed hostile. I did not tell my father, who would bring me back home every Saturday evening. I never complained.

But he must have understood, because in the Easter holidays, his sister, whose husband had opened a bakery in Nantes, suddenly came to see us and I realized that a plan had been hatched through letters.

My aunt, who had a very pink complexion, was starting to thicken out. She had no children, which was a source of distress to her.

For several days, she hovered awkwardly around me as if to tame me.

She told me about Nantes, their house near the harbour, the nice smell of bread, her husband who spent all night in his bakehouse and slept during the day.

She was very cheerful. I had guessed. I was resigned. Or more precisely, because I do not like that word, I accepted.

My father and I had a long conversation, walking in the country one Sunday morning after mass. It was the first time he had spoken to me as if I was a man. We talked about my future, how there was no way I could study in the village, and how, if I remained a boarder, I would lack a normal family life.

I know now what he was thinking. He realized that the company of a man like him, who had withdrawn into himself and lived mostly with his own thoughts, was not desirable for a boy who still expected everything of life.

I left with my aunt, a big trunk jogging up and down behind us, in the cart that took us to the railway station.

My father shed no tears. Neither did I.

That is pretty much all I know about him. For years, in Nantes, I was the baker's nephew, and I almost became accustomed to the man whose hairy chest I saw every day in the glowing light of the oven.

I spent all my holidays with my father. I would not go so far as to say that we were strangers to each other. But I had my own life, my own ambitions, my own problems.

He was my father, and I loved and respected him, but I was no longer trying to understand him. And that lasted for years. Is it always like that? I'm inclined to think it is.

By the time I became curious again, it was too late to ask the questions I would so much have liked to ask, the questions I blamed myself for not asking when he was still there to answer them.

My father had died at the age of forty-four, of pleurisy.

I was a young man, and had already started my medical studies. The last few times I had gone to the chateau, I had been struck by how pink my father's cheeks were, how shiny and feverish his eyes became in the evening.

'Are there consumptives in the family?' I asked my aunt one day.

'No, of course not!' she replied, as if I had spoken about a shameful vice. 'They were all as strong as oak trees! Don't you remember your grandfather?'

Actually, I did. I remembered a particular dry cough that he would put down to tobacco. And as far back as I could remember, I saw my father's cheeks looking as if the same fire was smouldering beneath them.

My aunt too had those pink flushes.

'From always living in the heat of a bakery!' she would retort.

She nevertheless died, ten years later, of the same illness as her brother.

As for me, when I got back to Nantes, where I had to go to pick up my things before beginning a new life, I hesitated for a long time then presented myself at the home of one of my teachers and asked him to examine me.

'No danger of that!' he reassured me.

Two days later, I took the train for Paris.

This time, my wife will not begrudge me returning to the subject of Simenon and the image he has created of me, because I need to discuss a point he raised in one of his recent books, a point that particularly touches me.

It is even one of the points that has most bothered me – far more than the small matter of clothes or other things I have amused myself raising.

I would not be my father's son if I was not touchy about my profession, my career, and that is what I want to talk about now.

I have sometimes had the impression, a disagreeable impression, that Simenon was trying in a way to apologize for me to the public for having joined the police. And I am sure that, in the minds of some, I could only ever have seen that profession as second best.

There is certainly no doubt that I started studying medicine, a profession I chose of my own free will, without being forced into it by more or less ambitious parents, as is often the case.

I had not thought about it for years, nor did I even think of tackling the matter, but precisely because of a few sentences written about my vocation, the subject has gradually asserted itself.

I have not talked about it to anyone, not even my wife. Today, I will have to overcome a certain modesty on my part to make things clear, or try to.

In one of his books, then, Simenon spoke of a 'mender of destinies'. He did not invent the phrase. It is indeed mine, and he must have heard me use it one day when we were having a friendly chat.

I wonder if it did not all start with Gadelle, whose tragedy, I have realized subsequently, had made a greater impression on me than I had thought.

Because he was a doctor, because he had failed, the medical profession began to assume an extraordinary prestige in my eyes, to the point of becoming a kind of priesthood.

For years, without realizing it, I tried to understand the tragedy of that man, who had grappled with a destiny he could not measure up to.

And I remembered my father's attitude towards him. I wondered if my father had understood the same thing as me, and if that was why, whatever it cost him, he had let him try his luck.

From Gadelle, imperceptibly, I went on to most of the people I had known, simple people most of them, leading apparently straightforward lives, but who nevertheless had eventually had to confront their own destinies.

Let us not forget that these are not the thoughts of a mature man I am trying to transcribe here, but rather the thought process in the mind of a young boy, and then of an adolescent.

My mother's death seemed to me such a stupid, such a *pointless* tragedy!

And all the other tragedies I had known, all those failures, plunged me into a kind of angry despair.

Was it impossible to do anything about it? Did we simply have to accept that there did not exist a man more intelligent or more informed than everybody else – a man I saw more or less in the guise of a family doctor, a Gadelle who had not failed – capable of saying gently but firmly:

'You've taken a wrong turning. By acting in that way, you're bound for disaster. Your real place is here and not there.'

That is it, I think: I had the obscure feeling that too many people were not in their rightful places, that they were making an effort to play roles they were not suited to, and that consequently, the game, for them, was lost in advance.

I really do not want it to be thought that I had any pretensions to one day become that kind of God the Father.

Having tried to understand Gadelle, then to understand my father's behaviour towards him, I continued to look around me and ask myself the same questions.

Here is an example that may be amusing. One year, there were fifty-eight of us in my class, fifty-eight pupils from different backgrounds, with different qualities, ambitions and faults. I amused myself imagining what I thought of as the ideal fates of all my classmates. In my mind, I called them, 'The lawyer . . . The tax collector . . .'

I also strove for a while to guess how the people close to me would eventually die.

Is it more understandable now why I had the idea of becoming a doctor? The word *police*, at that time, conjured up for me only the uniformed officer at the corner of the street. And although I may have heard of the secret police, I did not have the faintest idea what it might be.

Now, suddenly, I had to earn my living. I arrived in Paris without even a vague notion of the career I was going to choose. Given my unfinished studies, I could hardly hope to find anything other than office work, and it was in that spirit, although without enthusiasm, that I started reading the small ads in the newspapers. My uncle had suggested keeping me on in the bakery and teaching me his trade, but to no avail.

In the little hotel where I lodged on the Left Bank, there lived on the same landing as me a man who intrigued me, a man in his forties in whom I saw, God knows why, a certain resemblance to my father.

Physically, he was as different as possible from the thin fair-haired man with drooping shoulders whom I had always seen in leather gaiters.

This man was short and stocky, with brown hair. He was going prematurely bald, which he concealed by carefully bringing his hair forward, and he had a small black moustache, the ends of which he curled with an iron.

He was always dressed very respectably in black, wore an overcoat with a velvet collar (which explains a certain other overcoat), and carried a cane with a solid silver pommel.

I think the resemblance to my father lay in his bearing, in a certain way of walking without ever hurrying, of looking and listening and then somehow withdrawing into himself.

I met him by chance in a local fixed-price restaurant. I learned that he had his evening meal there almost every day, and for no particular reason I started to feel that I wanted to make his acquaintance.

I tried in vain to guess what his job was. He was most likely a bachelor, since he was living alone in the hotel. I heard him get up in the morning and come back in the evening at irregular hours.

He never had any visitors, and the one time I met him in company he was in conversation, on the corner of Boulevard Saint-Michel, with an individual so dubious-looking that one would have had no hesitation, at the time, in calling him a member of an apache gang.

I was on the verge of finding a place in a lacemaking firm in Rue des Victoires. I was due to go there the following day with references I had requested in writing from my former teachers.

That evening, in the restaurant, driven by some instinct or other, I made up my mind to get up from the table just as my neighbour was putting his napkin back in its pigeon-hole, so that I found myself holding the door open for him.

He must have noticed me before. Perhaps he had guessed how much I wanted to speak to him, because he now looked at me intently.

'Thank you,' he said.

Then, as I was standing there on the pavement:

'Are you going back to the hotel?'

'I think so . . . I don't know . . .'

It was a fine night in late autumn. The banks of the river were not far, and you could see the moon rising above the trees.

'Alone in Paris?'

'I'm alone, yes.'

Without asking for my company, he accepted it, took it as a given.

'Are you looking for work?'

'How did you know?'

He did not trouble to reply and slipped a cachou into his mouth. I was soon to understand why. He suffered from bad breath and knew it.

'Are you from the provinces?'

'From Nantes, but I was born in the country.'

I felt quite confident, talking to him. It was more or less the first time, since I had arrived in Paris, that I had found a companion, and his silence did not bother me at all, no doubt because I was accustomed to my father's benevolent silences.

I had told him almost my whole life story by the time we found ourselves on Quai des Orfèvres, on the other side of the Pont Saint-Michel.

He stopped in front of a big half-open door and said, 'Do you mind waiting? I'll only be a few minutes.'

A uniformed policeman was on duty at the door. After walking up and down for a while, I asked him, 'Isn't this the Palais de Justice?'

'This entrance is to the premises of the Sûreté.'

My neighbour's name was Jacquemain. He was indeed a bachelor, as I was to learn as we strolled by the Seine that night, crossing the same bridges several times, almost always with the mass of the Palais de Justice looming over us.

He was a police inspector, and he spoke to me about his profession, as briefly as my father would have done about his, and with the same underlying pride.

He was killed three years later, before I myself had started working in those offices on Quai des Orfèvres which had assumed such prestige for me. It happened somewhere over towards Porte d'Italie, in the course of a brawl. A bullet which was not even intended for him hit him full in the chest.

His photograph is still there, with others, in one of those black frames surmounted by the words 'Killed on duty.'

He did not talk much. Mainly, he listened to me. Which did not prevent me, at about eleven that night, from asking him in a voice trembling with impatience, 'Do you really think it's possible?'

'I'll give you an answer tomorrow evening.'

Obviously I could not go straight into the Sûreté. It was not yet the days of diplomas, and everyone had to work their way up through the ranks.

My only ambition was to be accepted, in any position, in one of the police stations of Paris, to be allowed to discover for myself an aspect of the world that Inspector Jacquemain had merely allowed me to glimpse.

As we parted on the landing in our hotel, which has since been demolished, he asked me, 'Would you mind very much having to wear a uniform?'

I gave a little start, I admit, a short hesitation which did not escape him and which could not have pleased him.

'No . . .' I replied in a low voice.

And I did wear one, not for long, seven or eight months. Since I had long legs and was very thin and very fast – strange as that may seem today – I was given a bicycle and, in order to teach me to get to know Paris, a city where I was still constantly getting lost, I was entrusted with the task of delivering messages to the various offices.

Has Simenon ever written about that? I do not recall. For months, perched on my bicycle, I weaved my way between the carriages and the omnibuses, still horse-drawn, which, especially when they hurtled down from Montmartre, scared me to death.

The officials still wore frock coats and top hats and, from a certain rank upwards, morning coats.

The policemen, for the most part, were men of a certain age, often with red noses, whom you would see drinking at zinc counters with coachmen, and of whom the cabaret singers made fun shamelessly.

I was not married. My uniform made me embarrassed about courting girls, and I decided that my real life would only begin the day I entered the 'house' on Quai des Orfèvres, no longer as a messenger bearing official notes, but as an inspector, by the main staircase.

When I spoke to him of this ambition, my neighbour did not smile, but looked at me with a thoughtful air and murmured, 'Why not?'

I did not know that I would go to his funeral so soon. My prognoses about human destinies still left a lot to be desired.

4.

In which I eat Anselme and Géraldine's petits fours under the noses of the Highways Department

Did my father or my grandfather ever ask themselves if they could have been anything other than what they were? Had they had other ambitions? Did they envy other people whose fates were different from theirs?

It is strange to have lived for so long with people and to know nothing of what today would seem essential. I have often asked myself the question, feeling as I do that I have straddled two worlds that are completely alien to one another.

Simenon and I talked about this not so long ago in my apartment on Boulevard Richard-Lenoir. It may have been on the eve of his departure for the United States. He had lingered in front of the enlarged photograph of my father, although he had seen it for years on the wall of the dining room.

Examining it with particular attention, he threw me searching little glances, as if trying to establish comparisons. It seemed to have made him thoughtful.

'When it comes down to it, Maigret,' he finally said, 'you were born in the ideal surroundings, at the ideal moment in the evolution of a family, to become a top-ranking functionary, a civil servant.'

That struck me, because I had already thought about it, in a less specific and above all less personal fashion, having noted the number of my colleagues who came from peasant families that had only recently lost direct contact with the land.

'I'm ahead by a generation,' Simenon continued, almost with an air of regret, as if he envied me. 'I have to go back to my grandfather to find an equivalent to your father. My father was already at the functionary stage.'

My wife was looking at him attentively, making an effort to understand.

'Normally I should have attained the liberal professions by the back door, from below,' he went on in a lighter tone. 'I should have struggled to become a neighbourhood doctor, a lawyer, an engineer. Or else . . .'

'Or else what?'

'Become embittered, a rebel. That's the majority, inevitably. Otherwise, there would be a surfeit of doctors and lawyers. I think I'm from the stock that provides the largest number of failures.'

I have no idea why this conversation has suddenly come back to me. It is probably because I am writing about my early years and trying to analyse my state of mind at the time.

I was alone in the world. I had just arrived in a Paris I did not know, a Paris where wealth was displayed more ostentatiously than it is today.

Two things stood out: that wealth, on one side, and on the other side, poverty. And I was on the latter side.

There was a world that led a life of refined idleness while the crowd looked on. The newspapers reported all the doings of these people who had no concerns other than their pleasures and their vanities.

Never for a moment was I tempted to rebel. I did not envy them. I did not hope to be like them one day. I did not compare my lot with theirs.

As far as I was concerned, they were part of a world as different as that of another planet.

I remember that in those days I had an insatiable appetite, which was already legendary when I was a child. In Nantes, my aunt liked to tell about how she had seen me come in from school and eat a two-kilo loaf of bread, which had not prevented me from having dinner two hours later.

I was earning very little money, and my great concern was to satisfy that appetite. For me, luxury was not what appeared on the terraces of the famous boulevard cafés, or in the shop windows of Rue de la Paix, but, more prosaically, in the pork butchers' displays.

On the routes I habitually took, I knew a certain number of pork butchers' shops that fascinated me, and in the days when I still rode around Paris on my bicycle, I would calculate my time in order to gain the few minutes I needed to buy a piece of sausage or a slice of pâté from them and eat it in the street, along with a roll bought from the bakery next door.

My stomach assuaged, I felt happy, full of self-confidence. I was doing my job conscientiously. I attached importance to the slightest tasks that were entrusted to me. There was no question of overtime. As far as I was concerned, all my time belonged to the police, and it struck me as quite natural that I should be kept working fourteen or fifteen hours in a row.

I do not say this to give myself credit. On the contrary: as far as I can recall, it was a state of mind that was common at the time.

Few policeman had had more than an elementary education. Thanks to Inspector Jacquemain, it was known in the upper echelons – although I myself was as yet unaware who knew, or even that anybody knew – that I had started my further education.

After a few months, I was quite surprised to see myself appointed to a post that struck me as quite unexpected: that of secretary to the chief inspector of a police station in the Saint-Georges district.

It was, however, a post that was not highly regarded at the time. A station secretary was known as the chief's dog.

My bicycle, my helmet and my uniform were taken away from me, as was the possibility of stopping at a pork butcher's in the course of my errands in the streets of Paris.

I particularly appreciated the fact that I was now in plain clothes the day I heard a voice calling out to me as I walked along Boulevard Saint-Michel.

A tall young man in a white coat was running after me.

'Jubert!' I cried.

'Maigret!'

'What are you doing here?'

'What about you? . . . Listen. I daren't stay outside now. Come and see me at seven o'clock in front of the pharmacy.'

Jubert, Félix Jubert, had been one of my classmates at the school of medicine in Nantes. I knew that he had given up his studies at the same time as me, but I think for other reasons. Without being a dunce, he was quite slow, and I remember that it was said of him:

'He studies until the cows come home, but he's forgotten it all the next day.'

He was very tall and thin, with a large nose, coarse features and red hair. Ever since I had known him his face had always been covered, not with those little acne spots that are the despair of young men, but with big red or purple spots to which he was constantly applying ointments and medicinal powders.

That same evening, I went and waited for him outside the pharmacy where he had been working for several weeks. He had no family in Paris. He was living around the Cherche-Midi, with people who took in two or three lodgers.

'What about you, what are you doing?'

'I've joined the police.'

I can still see his purple eyes, as clear as a young girl's, trying to hide his incredulity. His voice sounded quite strange as he repeated, 'The police?'

He looked at my suit, then, despite himself, at the policeman on duty at the corner of the boulevard, as if to establish a comparison.

'I'm secretary to a chief inspector.'

'Oh, right! I understand!'

Whether out of human respect, or because of my inability to explain myself and his inability to understand, I did not admit to him that just three weeks earlier, I had still been wearing a uniform and my ambition had been to join the Sûreté.

In his eyes, in the eyes of many people, secretary was a perfectly honourable position. I was neat and tidy, I worked in an office, surrounded by books, with a pen in my hand.

'Do you have many friends in Paris?'

Apart from Inspector Jacquemain, I knew virtually nobody, because I was still a newcomer at the station, and people were wary of opening up to me.

'No girl either? What do you do with all your free time?'

Firstly, I did not have much. Secondly, I was studying, because, in order to reach my goal more quickly, I had decided to take the exams that had just been introduced.

We had dinner together that evening. As we were having dessert, he said to me, with a promising air:

'I'll have to introduce you.'

'Who to?'

'To some nice people. Friends. You'll see.'

He did not say anything more that first day. I no longer know why, but we did not see each other again for several weeks. We might not have seen each other again at all. I had not given him my address and I did not have his. It did not even occur to me to go and wait for him outside his pharmacy.

It was chance that brought us together again, at the door of the Théâtre-Français, where we were both queueing.

'It's stupid!' he said. 'I thought I'd lost you. I don't even know which station you're working in. I told my friends about you.'

He had a way of talking about those friends which might have made one think that it was some kind of special clan, even a mysterious sect.

'Do you at least have a tailcoat?'

'I have one.'

There was no point in adding that it was my father's – somewhat old-fashioned in style, since he had worn it at his wedding – and that I had had it altered to my size.

'I'll take you on Friday. Make sure you're free without fail on Friday evening at eight o'clock. Can you dance?'

'No.'

'It doesn't matter. But it wouldn't be a bad idea if you took a few lessons. I know a good course that's not too expensive. I went there myself.'

This time, he made a note of my address and even of the little restaurant where I was in the habit of having dinner when I was not on duty, and on Friday evening he was in my room, sitting on my bed, as I got dressed.

'I'd better explain so you don't make any blunders. You and I will be the only ones there who don't work as engineers for the Highways Department. A distant cousin of mine, whom I met again by chance, introduced me. Monsieur and Madame Léonard are charming people, and their niece is the most delightful girl.'

I immediately grasped that he was in love with her and that it was to show me the object of his ardour that he was dragging me there.

'Don't worry, there are others,' he promised. 'Some really nice ones.'

As it was raining and it was very important not to arrive spattered with mud, we took a carriage, the first carriage I had taken in Paris for other than professional reasons. I can still see our white shirt fronts as we passed the gas lamps. And I still see Félix Jubert stopping the carriage outside a florist's shop to buy something to adorn our buttonholes.

'Old Monsieur Léonard,' he explained, 'Anselme his name is, has been retired for about ten years. Before that, he was one of the most highly placed officials in the Highways Department, and his successors sometimes still consult him. His niece's father also works for the Highways Department. So do pretty much the whole family.'

From the way he talked about the Highways Department, it was obvious that for Jubert it was some kind of lost paradise, and that he would have given anything not to have wasted precious years studying medicine and to be able to work there too.

'You'll see!'

And I did. We came to an old but comfortable and even opulent-looking building on Boulevard Beaumarchais, not far from Place de la Bastille. All the windows on the first floor were lit, and from Jubert's look as we got out of the carriage it was clear to me that it was there that the announced festivities were going to take place.

I did not feel very comfortable. I regretted having let myself be dragged along. My wing collar bothered me. I had the impression that my cravat was constantly getting knocked sideways, and that one of the tails of my coat had a tendency to rise up like a rooster's crest.

The staircase was dimly lit, the steps covered with a crimson carpet that struck me as sumptuous. And the windows on the landing were of stained glass, which for a long time I considered the last word in refinement.

Jubert had spread a thicker than usual layer of ointment on his pimply face, and for some reason that gave him a purple tinge. He pulled reverently on a large soft tassel that hung in front of a door. From inside, we could hear a murmur of conversation, with that touch of sharpness in the voices and the laughter that indicates the animation of a social gathering.

A maid in a white apron opened the door, and Jubert held out his coat, happy to utter, as one familiar with the place, 'Good evening, Clémence.'

'Good evening, Monsieur Félix.'

The drawing room was quite large and not very well lit, with a profusion of dark hangings, and in the next room, visible through a wide picture window, the furniture had been pushed back against the walls in order to leave the parquet floor free for dancing.

Jubert led me protectively to an old lady with white hair sitting beside the fireplace.

'May I introduce my friend Maigret, whom I've had the honour to mention to you, and who has been dying to pay his respects to you personally.'

He had probably repeated this sentence to himself all the way there, and he made sure that I bowed correctly, that I was not too awkward, and that I was indeed doing him proud.

The old lady was delightful – short, with fine features and a lively face – but I was thrown when she said to me with a smile:

'Why aren't you in the Highways Department? I'm sure Anselme will be sorry.'

Her name was Géraldine. Her husband Anselme was sitting in another armchair, so motionless that he seemed to have been carried there to be displayed like a wax figure. He was very old. I learned later that he was well over eighty and that Géraldine had also reached the age of eighty.

Someone was playing the piano softly: a large young man who seemed to be bursting from his tailcoat. A young girl dressed in pale blue was turning the pages for him. She had her back to me. When I was introduced to her, I did not dare look her in the face, so disconcerted was I at being there, so uncertain as to what to say or where to put myself.

The dancing had not started yet. On a pedestal table there was a tray of petits fours, and some time later, as Jubert had abandoned me to my fate, I approached it, I still do not know why – not out of greed, certainly, because I was not hungry and I have never liked petits fours – probably to put up a front.

I took one mechanically. Then another. Someone said, 'Shh!'

And a second girl, this one in pink, with a slight squint, started singing, standing by the piano, on which she supported herself with one hand while waving a fan with the other.

I was still eating. I did not even realize it, any more than I realized that the old lady was watching me in astonishment, or that others, noticing what I was doing, found it hard to take their eyes off me.

One of the young men made a remark under his breath to his cousin and we again heard, 'Shhh!'

You could count the young girls by the bright splashes of colour amid the black tailcoats. There were four of them. Jubert was apparently trying to attract my attention without success, unhappy to see me grab the petits fours one by one and conscientiously eat them. He confessed to me later that he had felt sorry for me, being convinced that I had not had dinner.

Others must have thought the same. The song was over. Everyone clapped, and the girl in pink acknowledged the applause. It was then that I noticed that I was the one everybody was looking at, standing as I was beside the pedestal table with my mouth full, a little cake in my hand.

I was on the verge of leaving without an apology, of beating a retreat, literally fleeing that apartment in which a world that was totally alien to me had its being.

At that moment, in the dim light, I noticed a face, the face of the girl in blue, and, on that face, a gentle, reassuring, almost familiar expression. It was as if she had understood and was encouraging me.

The maid came in with refreshments, and after having eaten so much so inopportunely, I did not dare take a glass when it was offered to me.

'Louise, you should pass the petits fours.'

That was how I discovered that the girl in blue was named Louise and that she was the niece of Monsieur and Madame Léonard.

She served everyone before approaching me and, pointing to some cakes with little pieces of crystallized fruit on them, said with a conspiratorial air, 'They've left the best. Taste these.'

All I could find to say in reply was, 'Do you think so?'

They were the first words Madame Maigret and I ever exchanged.

In a while, when she reads what I am writing, I know perfectly well that she will shrug her shoulders and say, 'What's the point of talking about that?'

Deep down, she is delighted with the image Simenon has given of her, the image of a nice old 'granny', always cooking, always polishing, always pampering her big baby of a husband. I suspect it was actually because of that image that she was the first to establish a real friendship with him, to the point of considering him part of the family and defending him even when I had no intention of attacking him.

The fact is, like all portraits, it is far from accurate. When I met her, on that famous evening, she was a somewhat plump, fresh-faced girl with a gleam in her eyes that was not to be seen in those of her friends.

What would have happened if I had not eaten those cakes? It is quite possible she would not have noticed me among the dozen young men who were there and who all, apart from my friend Jubert, worked for the Highways Department.

Those words 'Highways Department' have retained an almost comical meaning for us, and someone has just to say them to make us smile. If we hear them somewhere, even now, we cannot help giving each other knowing looks.

The correct thing now would be to present the whole family tree of the Schoellers, the Kurts and the Léonards, which confused me for a long time, and which constitutes my wife's side of the family.

If you go to Alsace, anywhere from Strasbourg to Mulhouse, you will probably hear of them. It was, I believe, a Kurt from Scharrachbergheim who, under Napoleon, was the first to establish the almost dynastic tradition of working on roads and bridges. Apparently he was famous in his time, and allied himself with the Schoellers, who worked for the same department.

The Léonards later also joined the family, and since then, from father to son, from brother to brother-in-law or cousin, everyone, or almost everyone, has belonged to the same profession, to the point that when a Kurt became one of the biggest brewers in Colmar it was considered a comedown.

I had only a slight inkling of all this that evening, thanks to the few indications that Jubert had given me.

And when we left, in the pouring rain, neglecting this time to take a carriage, which in any case we would have had some difficulty finding in that neighbourhood, I myself almost felt some regret that I had chosen the wrong career.

'What do you think of her?'

'Who?'

'Louise! I don't blame you. All the same, the situation was embarrassing. You saw how tactfully she put you at your ease, without seeming to? She's a remarkable girl. Alice Perret is more brilliant, but . . .'

I had no idea who Alice Perret was. The only person I had met the whole evening was the girl in blue, who had come and chatted to me between dances.

'Alice is the one who sang. I think she's soon going to become engaged to the young man who accompanied her, Louis, whose parents are very rich.'

We did not part until very late that night. Every time there was another shower, we entered some bistro that was still open to take shelter and have coffee. Félix would not let me go, but talked endlessly about Louise, trying to force me to admit that she was the ideal girl.

'I know I don't stand much of a chance. It's because her parents would like to find her a husband who's in the Highways Department that they've sent her to stay with her uncle Léonard. You understand, there's no one available in Colmar or in Mulhouse, or else they're already part of the family. She's been here for two months. She's supposed to be spending the whole winter in Paris.'

'Does she know that?'

'What?

'That they're trying to find her a husband in the Highways Department.'

'Of course. But she doesn't care. She has a mind of her own, much more than you may think. You haven't had time to appreciate her. Next Friday, you should try talking to her a bit more. If you could dance, it'd be a lot easier. Why don't you take two or three lessons between now and then?'

I did not take any dance lessons. Fortunately. Because Louise, contrary to what good old Jubert thought, hated nothing more than whirling around the room on the arm of a dance partner.

It was two weeks later that a little incident took place to which, at the time, I attached great importance – and which may actually have been important, but in a different way.

The young engineers who came to the Léonards formed a separate gang, and affected among themselves a special language that meant nothing outside the members of their brotherhood.

Did I hate them? It is likely that I did. And I did not like the way they insisted on calling me inspector. It had become a game, and I was weary of it.

'Hey, inspector!' they would call from one end of the drawing room to the other.

On this particular occasion, as Jubert and Louise were chatting in a corner, near a pot plant – I can still see it – a young man in glasses approached them and confided something to them in a low voice, throwing an amused glance in my direction.

A few moments later, I asked Jubert, 'What did he say?'

To which, embarrassed, he replied evasively, 'Nothing.'

'Something nasty?'

'I'll tell you outside.'

The young man with the glasses did the same thing in other groups, and everyone seemed to be amusing themselves greatly at my expense.

Everyone except Louise, who, that evening, refused several dances, which she spent talking to me.

Once outside, I questioned Jubert.

'What did he say?'

'First of all, answer me frankly. What did you do before becoming the inspector's secretary?'

'Well . . . I was in the police . . .'

'In uniform?'

So that was it! The fellow in the glasses must have recognized me from having seen me in my policeman's uniform.

Just imagine, a policeman among these gentlemen from the Highways Department!

'What did Louise say?' I asked, with a catch in my throat.

'She was very decent. She's always very decent. You won't believe me, but you'll see . . .'

Poor old Jubert!

'She told him the uniform must have suited you better than it would have suited him.'

All the same, I did not go to Boulevard Beaumarchais the following Friday. I avoided meeting Jubert. It was he who came to relaunch things with me two weeks later.

'You know, we were worried about you last Friday.'

'Who?'

'Madame Léonard. She asked me if you were ill.'

'I was very busy.'

I was sure that, if Madame Léonard had spoken about me, it was because her niece . . .

Anyway, I do not see much point in going into all these details. I am already going to find it hard enough to make sure that what I have just written does not end up in the waste-paper basket.

For nearly three months, Jubert played his role without suspecting a thing, and without our trying in any way to deceive him. It was he who would come to fetch me from my hotel and tie my cravat on the pretext that I did not know how to dress. It was he who would say to me, when he saw me alone in a corner of the drawing room:

'You should speak to Louise. You're not being polite.'

It was he who, when we left, always insisted:

'You're wrong to think she isn't interested in you. On the contrary, she likes you very much. She always asks me questions about you.'

Towards Christmas, the girl who squinted became engaged to the pianist, and they were no longer seen on Boulevard Beaumarchais.

I do not know if Louise's attitude was beginning to discourage the others, or if we had been less discreet than we thought we were. The fact remains that, every Friday, there were fewer and fewer people in Anselme and Géraldine's apartment.

The big heart to heart with Jubert took place in February, in my room. That Friday, he was not in evening dress, I noticed it immediately. He had the bitter, resigned air associated with certain leading roles at the Comédie Française.

'Even so, I still came to tie a knot in your cravat!' he said with a grimace.

'Aren't you free?'

'Oh, I'm completely free, as free as the air, freer than I've ever been before.'

And, standing in front of me, my white cravat in his hand, his eyes looking straight into mine:

'Louise has told me everything.'

I was flabbergasted. Because she had not yet said anything to me. Nor had I said anything to her.

'What are you talking about?'

'You and she.'

'But—'

'I asked her the question. I went to see her yesterday, specially.'

'What question?'

'I asked her if she wanted to marry me.'

'Did she say no?'

'She said no. She said she liked me a lot, that I'll always be her best friend, but that—'

'Did she talk to you about me?'

'Not exactly.'

'What, then?'

'I understood! I should have understood right from the first evening, when you ate those petits fours and she looked at you so indulgently. When women look indulgently at a man who behaves the way you were behaving . . .'

Poor Jubert! We lost touch with him almost immediately, just as we lost touch with all those gentlemen from the Highways Department, apart from Uncle Léonard.

For years, we never knew what had become of him. I was nearly fifty when one day, on the Canebière in Marseilles, I went into a pharmacy to buy some aspirin. I had not read the name on the shopfront. I heard an exclamation:

'Maigret!'

'Jubert!'

'What are you up to these days? No, that's a stupid question, I've long known what you're up to, thanks to the newspapers. How's Louise?'

Then he told me about his eldest son, who, by a gentle irony of fate, was preparing his exam to get into the Highways Department.

With Jubert missing at Boulevard Beaumarchais, the Friday parties became even more poorly attended, and there was often now nobody to play the piano. On those occasions, it was Louise who played, and I turned the pages while a couple or two danced in the dining room, which had grown too large.

I do not think I asked Louise if she wanted to marry me. Most of the time, we spoke about my career, the police, the profession of inspector.

I told her how much I would earn when I was at last appointed to Quai des Orfèvres, adding that it would take at least another three years, and that until then, my income would be insufficient to maintain a household with dignity.

I also told her about the two or three conversations I had had with Xavier Guichard, already the chief, who had not forgotten my father and had more or less taken me under his wing.

'I don't know if you like Paris. Because you do realize I'll be obliged to spend my whole life in Paris?'

'But we can live as quietly here as in the provinces, can't we?'

At last, one Friday, none of the guests was there, only Géraldine, who opened the door to me herself, dressed in black silk, and said to me with a certain solemnity, 'Come in!'

Louise was not in the drawing room. There were no trays of cakes, no refreshments. Spring had come, and there was no fire in the hearth. It seemed to me that there was nothing to cling on to. I had kept my hat in my hand, embarrassed by my tailcoat and my polished shoes.

'Tell me, young man, what are your intentions?'

It was probably one of the most difficult moments of my life. Her voice struck me as brusque and accusatory. I did not dare raise my eyes. Looking down at the leaf-patterned carpet, all I could see was the hem of a black dress, with the end of a very pointed shoe sticking out. My ears turned red.

'I swear to you . . .' I stammered.

'I'm not asking you to swear. I'm asking if you intend to marry her.'

I looked at her at last, and I do not think I have ever seen an old woman's face express so much affectionate mischief.

'Of course!'

Apparently – or so I have been told subsequently – I sprang up like a jack-in-the-box and repeated in an even louder voice:

'Of course I do!'

And almost yelled, a third time:

'Of course, for heaven's sake!'

She did not even raise her voice to call: 'Louise!'

Louise, who had been standing behind a half-open door, now came in, quite shyly, her face as red as mine.

'What did I tell you?' her aunt asked.

'Why?' I cut in. 'Didn't you believe it?'

'I wasn't sure. It was my aunt . . .'

Let us move on, because I am convinced the marital censorship board would cut the passage anyway.

As for old Léonard, I have to say that he showed less enthusiasm and never forgave me for not belonging to the Highways Department. Almost a hundred years old, rooted to his armchair by his infirmities, he would shake his head as he looked at me, as if there was something not quite right about the way the world functioned these days.

'You'll have to take some leave to go to Colmar. What about the Easter holidays?'

It was old Géraldine who wrote to Louise's parents, several times – to prepare them for the shock, as she put it – announcing the news to them.

At Easter, I was given just forty-eight hours' leave. I spent most of it on trains, which were not as fast then as they are now.

I was received correctly, without much enthusiasm.

'The best way to know if your intentions are serious is to keep away from each other for a while. Louise will stay here this summer. In the autumn you can come back and see us.'

'Am I allowed to write to her?'

'As long as you don't overdo it. Once a week, for example.'

It seems funny now. It certainly was not at the time.

I had vowed, without any ulterior motive, to have Jubert as my best man. When I went to see him at the pharmacy on Boulevard Saint-Michel, he was no longer there, and nobody knew what had become of him.

I spent part of the summer looking for an apartment and found the one on Boulevard Richard-Lenoir.

'Just until something better comes along, you understand? When I'm made an inspector . . .'

5.

Which deals in a somewhat incoherent fashion with hobnailed boots, apaches, prostitutes, hot-air vents, pavements and railway stations

Some years ago now, some of us came up with the idea of starting a kind of club, more like a monthly dinner, which was to be called the Hobnailed Boots Dinner. We met for an aperitif at the Brasserie Dauphine to discuss who should or should not be allowed to join, including a quite serious debate about whether those from the other house – Rue des Saussaies – would be eligible.

Then, as was to be expected, things got no further. At the time, there were at least four of us, among the chief inspectors in the Police Judiciaire, to take a certain pride in the name 'Hobnailed Boots', which used to be applied to us by cabaret singers, and which some young inspectors just out of the academy sometimes use among themselves about those veterans who have been through the mill.

The truth of it is that in the old days it took many years to earn one's stripes, and exams were not enough. An inspector could not hope for promotion until he had slogged away in pretty much all the departments.

It is not easy to give the new generations a more or less accurate idea of what that meant.

'Hobnailed boots' and 'big moustaches': these words came quite naturally to people's lips when they talked about the police.

To be honest, I too, for years, wore hobnailed boots. Not because I liked them. And not, as the cartoonists seemed to insinuate, because we considered such footwear the height of elegance and comfort, but for more down-to-earth reasons.

Two reasons, to be precise. The first was that with the wages we earned, we could only just make ends meet. I often hear people talk about the joyful, carefree early years of the century. Young people cite the prices of that period with envy: Havana cigars for two sous, dinner with wine and coffee for twenty sous.

What is forgotten is that at the beginning of his career, a public official earned just under a hundred francs.

When I was on the beat, I would tramp kilometres and kilometres of pavement in a day – often a thirteen- or fourteen-hour day – and in all weathers.

So that the problem of resoling my shoes was one of our first problems as a married couple. When I brought my pay envelope to my wife at the end of the month, she would arrange its contents into a number of little piles.

'For the butcher . . . For the rent . . . For the gas . . .'

There was almost nothing left to make up the last pile of coins.

'For your shoes.'

The dream was always to buy new ones, but for a long time that remained merely a dream. Often I went for weeks without admitting to her that between the nails, my soles, which had become porous, greedily drank in the water from the gutters.

I mention this here, not out of resentment, but rather in a cheerful spirit, because I think it is necessary in order to give an idea of the life of an ordinary police officer.

There were no taxis, and even if the streets had been full of them they would have been inaccessible to us, as were the carriages we only used on rare occasions.

In any case, the job of a policeman on the beat was precisely to walk the pavement, to be part of the crowd, from morning to night or from night to morning.

Why, when I think about it, do I have, above all, a memory of rain? One might think that for years, all it did was rain, or that the seasons were not the same in those days. It is obviously because the rain added a number of extra tribulations to the job. It was not only your shoes that got drenched. There were the shoulders of your cape, which were gradually transformed into cold compresses, your hat which dripped, your hands which turned blue and which you thrust deep into your pockets.

The streets were less well lit than they are now. In the outlying parts of the city, some of them were not even paved. After nightfall, the windows were yellow squares in the darkness, houses still being largely lit by gas, or even, in the case of the poorer dwellings, by candle.

And then there were the apaches.

It was the fashion, in the shadowy area around the old city walls, for some young men to flash their knives around, and not always for profit, to steal respectable people's wallets or watches.

It was mainly a matter of proving to themselves that they were men, hard men, able to impress the young whores who plied their trade under the gas lamps in their pleated black skirts, their hair gathered into large buns.

We were not armed. Contrary to what the public imagines, a plainclothes policeman is not entitled to have a revolver in his pocket and if, in some cases, he does carry one, it is against regulations and he must take full responsibility for it.

Young officers could not afford that liberty. There were a certain number of streets, around La Villette, Ménilmontant and Porte d'Italie, which we would hesitate to enter, and where the noise of our own footsteps made our hearts pound.

A telephone, too, was for a long time beyond our means. If I happened to be delayed by several hours, there was no way I could call my wife to let her know, and she would spend solitary evenings under the light of the gas mantle in our dining room, listening out for sounds on the staircase and reheating the same dinner four or five times.

As for the moustaches given us by the cartoonists, they are also true. After all, a man without a moustache could easily pass for a servant.

I had rather a long, mahogany-coloured moustache, a little darker than my father's, with tapered ends. Subsequently, it got shorter, until it was no more than a toothbrush, before disappearing completely.

It is a fact that most of the inspectors had big black waxed moustaches, the kind you see in the cartoons. That is because over quite a long period of time, for some mysterious reason, the profession mainly attracted men from the Massif Central.

There are few streets in Paris I did not tramp, always on the alert, and I got to know all the street people: from the beggar, the organ grinder and the flower seller to the specialist in the three-card trick and the pickpocket, by way of the prostitute and the drunk old woman who spent most of her nights in police stations.

I 'did' Les Halles at night, Place Maubert, the riverbanks.

I also 'did' the crowds, which was a major task, at street fairs like the Foire du Trône and the Foire de Neuilly, the races at Longchamp, patriotic demonstrations, military parades, the visits of foreign monarchs, processions of coaches, travelling circuses, the flea market.

After a few months, a few years of this profession, you have an extensive repertoire of figures and faces in your head, and they stay engraved there for ever.

Difficult as it may be, I should like to give a more or less accurate idea of our relations with this clientele, including those we periodically found ourselves taking to the cells.

Needless to say, the picturesque aspect soon ceased to exist for us. Inevitably, we looked at the streets of Paris with a professional eye, which hooks on to certain familiar details, seizes this or that peculiarity and draws conclusions.

What strikes me most, as I write about this subject, are the bonds that develop between the policeman and those it is his job to track down. Above all, except in certain rare cases, there is an absolute absence of hatred in the policeman, or even of resentment.

An absence of pity, too, in the sense in which we generally use that word.

Our relations are, if you like, strictly professional.

As can easily be imagined, we see too much to be surprised any longer by some people's misfortunes or their perversions. We do not feel angry about the latter, but nor, when confronted by the former, does our heart bleed, as may happen to the uninformed layman.

What does exist, and what Simenon has tried unsuccessfully to convey, is, paradoxical as it may seem, a kind of family spirit.

Please do not think I am saying something I am not. We are on opposite sides of the barricade, that much is clear. But to a certain extent, we are also in the same boat.

The prostitute on Boulevard de Clichy and the inspector watching her both have bad shoes and aching feet after walking up and down kilometres of pavement. They have to suffer the same rain, the same icy wind. They both see the night in the same way, both have an identical insight into the hidden aspects of the crowd streaming past them.

It is the same in a fair where the pickpocket makes his way among this crowd. To him, a fair, or any gathering of some hundreds of individuals, means not enjoyment, wooden horses, circus tents, gingerbread, but a certain number of wallets in innocent pockets.

To the policeman, too. And both can spot at a glance the self-satisfied provincial who will make the ideal victim.

The number of times I followed some pickpocket of my acquaintance for hours on end! The one we called the

String, for example. He knew I was on his heels, watching everything he did. He knew that I knew. On my side, I knew that he knew I was there.

His job was to appropriate a wallet or a watch, despite everything, and mine was to stop him or to catch him in the act.

Well, the String would sometimes turn and smile at me, and I would smile back. He would sigh and say, 'It's going to be hard!'

I was not unaware that he was flat broke, that he would only eat that evening if he succeeded.

Nor was he unaware that I only earned a hundred francs a month, wore shoes with holes in them, and that my wife was waiting impatiently for me.

I arrested him at least ten times, with a pleasant 'Got you!'

And he was almost as relieved as I was. It meant that he would eat at the police station and sleep with a roof over his head. There are some who know the house so well that they ask, 'Who's on duty tonight?'

Because some people let them smoke and others do not.

For the next year and a half, I thought back to the pavements as an ideal place, because I had been assigned to the department stores.

Instead of the rain and the cold, the sun, the dust, I spent my days in an overheated atmosphere that smelled of Cheviot wool, unbleached cotton, linoleum and mercerized thread.

In those days, at intervals in the aisles between the counters, there were hot-air vents, which sent blasts of hot dry air up your body. That was really nice when you arrived wet. You would stand over a hot-air vent and immediately give off a cloud of steam.

After a few hours, you would prefer to remain near the doors, which let in a little oxygen each time they opened.

It was important to act naturally. To act as if you were a customer! Easier said than done, when a whole floor is filled with nothing but corsets, women's underwear or skeins of silk!

'Would you mind following me? Please don't make a fuss.'

Some understood immediately and went with us to the manager's office without a word. Others would react indignantly, start shouting, even throw a tantrum.

And yet here, too, we were dealing with a regular clientele. Whether at the Bon Marché, the Louvre or the Printemps, you would again see certain familiar faces, mostly middle-aged women who would stuff incredible amounts of merchandise into special pockets between their dresses and their petticoats.

Looking back now, a year and a half does not strike me as very long. At the time, each hour felt as long as an hour spent in a dentist's waiting room.

'Are you at the Galeries this afternoon?' my wife would sometimes ask me. 'I have to do a bit of shopping there.'

We did not speak. We pretended not to recognize each other. It was wonderful. I loved watching her as she walked brashly from counter to counter, occasionally throwing me a discreet wink.

I doubt she has ever asked herself if she could have married anyone other than a police inspector. She got to know the names of all my colleagues, spoke familiarly about those she had never seen, their obsessions, their successes and failures.

It took me years before I finally made up my mind, one Sunday morning when I was on duty, to introduce her to the famous house on Quai des Orfèvres. She was not surprised in any way. She walked about as if she were at home, searching out the details she knew so well by hearsay.

Her only reaction was: 'It's not as dirty as I imagined.'

'Why should it be dirty?'

'Places where there are only men are never all that clean. And they smell.'

I did not take her to the cells, where, as far as smells went, she would have had her fill.

'Whose seat is this here, on the left?'

'Torrence.'

'The really fat one? I should have guessed. He's like a child. He still enjoys carving his initials on the desk.

'What about the one who did all that walking, old Lagrume?'

Since I have spoken so much about shoes, I might as well tell the story that had moved my wife.

Lagrume, old Lagrume as we called him, was the eldest of us all, although he had never reached a rank above that of inspector. He was a tall, sad-looking man. In summer he suffered from hay fever, and as soon as it got cold again, his chronic bronchitis gave him a cavernous cough that could be heard from one end of the Police Judiciaire's offices to the other.

Fortunately, he was not often there. He had been careless enough to say one day, talking about his cough, 'My doctor has advised me to get a lot of fresh air.'

Since then, he had had his fill. He had long legs and big feet, and it was to him that we entrusted the most unlikely inquiries throughout Paris, those that oblige you to cross the city in all directions, day after day, without even the hope of a result.

'Just give it to Lagrume!'

Everyone knew what that meant, except the man himself, who would solemnly write down a few points in his notebook, take his rolled-up umbrella under his arm and leave after a little wave to everyone.

I wonder now if he was not perfectly aware of the role he was playing. He was resigned to his lot. For years and years, he had had a sick wife who waited for him to do the housework in their suburban home in the evenings. And when his daughter got married, I think it was he who would get up in the night to deal with the baby.

'Lagrume, you still smell of baby's poo!'

An old woman had been murdered in Rue Caulaincourt. It was a banal crime, which caused no stir in the press, because the victim was a woman with a small private income and no friends or family.

Those are almost always the most difficult cases. Confined to the department stores – and kept busy by the approach of Christmas – I did not have to deal with it, but like everyone in the house, I knew the details of the investigation.

The crime had been committed with the help of a kitchen knife, which had been left at the scene. That knife was the only clue. It was a perfectly ordinary knife, the kind sold in ironmongers', general stores and the smallest neighbourhood shops, and the manufacturer, who had been located, claimed that he had sold tens of thousands in the Paris region.

It was new. It had clearly been bought for the occasion. It still bore the price on the handle in indelible ink.

It was that detail that gave us a vague hope of finding the shopkeeper who had sold it.

'Lagrume! Deal with the knife.'

He wrapped it in a piece of newspaper, put it in his pocket and left.

He left for a journey through Paris that was to last nine weeks. Every morning, he continued to present himself on time in the office, and every evening, he would come back and put the knife away in a drawer. Every morning, you would see him put the weapon in his pocket, grab his umbrella and leave with the same wave to everyone.

I later found out the number of shops – the story has become legendary – that might have sold a knife of that kind. Without going beyond the fortifications, just keeping within the twenty arrondissements of Paris, it was breathtaking.

There was no question of using any kind of transport. It was a matter of going from street to street, almost from door to door. In his pocket, Lagrume had a map of Paris, on which, hour after hour, he would cross off a certain number of streets.

I think that by the end his superiors had forgotten which task they had given him.

'Is Lagrume available?'

Someone would answer that he was out on an assignment, and they would no longer bother to inquire about him. It was just before the holidays, as I have said. The winter was rainy and cold, and the streets slippery, and yet Lagrume continued to walk about with his bronchitis and his cavernous cough from morning to evening, never tiring, never wondering if it still had any meaning.

In the ninth week, well after New Year, when everything was frozen hard, they saw him come in at three in the afternoon, as calm and grim-faced as ever, without the slightest spark of joy or relief in his eyes.

'Is the chief here?'

'Did you find it?'

'I found it.'

Not in an ironmonger's, or a general store, or a shop selling household goods. He had been through them all in vain.

The knife had been sold by a stationer on Boulevard Rochechouart. The shopkeeper recognized his own handwriting and remembered a young man in a green scarf who had bought the weapon from him more than two months earlier.

He provided quite an accurate description, and the young man was arrested and executed the following year.

As for Lagrume, he died in the street, not from his bronchitis, but from a heart attack.

Before talking about railway stations, and especially about the Gare du Nord, with which it seems I have an old bone to pick, I must say a little about a subject I find somewhat disagreeable.

I have often been asked, when talking about my early days and my various posts, 'Were you ever in the vice squad?'

The fact is, I was, like most of my colleagues. Not for very long. Barely a few months.

And although I realize now that it was necessary, I nevertheless retain a memory of that period that is both vague and a little embarrassed.

I have spoken about the familiarity which naturally grows up between the police and those on whom it is their task to keep an eye.

By force of circumstance, it exists just as much in that area as in the others. Even more in that area. In fact, each inspector's clientele, if I can call it that, is composed of a relatively restricted number of women who are almost always found in the same places, at the door of the same hotel or under the same gas lamp, and for those of a slightly higher level, on the terraces of the same brasseries.

I did not yet have the solid build I have acquired with the years, and apparently I looked younger than my age.

Just recall the petits fours in that apartment on Boulevard Beaumarchais, and it should be obvious that, when it came to certain matters, I was somewhat shy.

Most officers in vice were on first-name terms with the girls. They knew not just their first names, but their nicknames too, and it was a tradition, when they loaded them into the Black Maria after a raid, to exchange the most foul-mouthed remarks, the most obscene and insulting words, laughing all the while.

Another habit these ladies had acquired was to pull up their skirts and show their backsides in a gesture they no doubt considered the ultimate insult, accompanied with words of defiance.

At the start, I sometimes blushed, because I still blushed quite easily. My embarrassment did not go unnoticed: the least one can say of these women is that they have a certain knowledge of men.

Consequently, I became, if not their pet hate, at the very least their whipping boy.

At Quai des Orfèvres, I have never been called by my first name, and I am convinced that a lot of my colleagues do not even know it . . . I would not have chosen it if I had been asked for my opinion. But nor am I ashamed of it.

Was it an act of revenge on the part of an inspector who knew it?

My main patch was the Sébastopol area, which, especially around Les Halles, was then frequented by a low class of prostitute, in particular a number of very old ones, whose refuge in a way it had become.

It was there, too, that young girls who had just arrived from Brittany or elsewhere learned their trade, so that you had the two extremes: sixteen-year-olds whom the pimps – popularly known as *Jules* – would fight over, and ageless harpies who could well take care of themselves.

One day, the refrain began – because it immediately became a refrain. I was passing one of these old women, who was standing at the door of a filthy hotel, when I heard her say, smiling through her rotten teeth:

'Good evening, Jules!'

I thought she had uttered the name off the top of her head, but a little further on I was greeted by similar words.

'Well, Jules?'

After which, whenever they were in a group, they would burst out laughing and make comments I cannot bring myself to write down.

I knew what some officers would have done in my place. They would have needed no other excuse to arrest a few of the women and lock them up in Saint-Lazare to think it over.

Making an example like that would have sufficed, and I would probably have been treated with a certain respect.

But I did not do so. Not necessarily out of a sense of justice. And not from pity either.

Probably because it was a game I did not want to play. I preferred to pretend that I had not heard. I hoped that they would tire of it. But those kinds of women are like children who can never have enough of a joke.

The famous Jules was put into a song which they started singing at the tops of their voices as soon as I appeared. Others would say, when I checked their cards:

'Don't be a swine, Jules! You're so cute!'

Poor Louise! Her great fear during that period was not that I would give in to temptation, but that I would bring a nasty illness into the house. I had already caught fleas. When I got home, she would make me undress and take a bath, while she went and brushed my clothes on the landing or outside the open window.

'You must have touched something today. Brush your nails carefully!'

Was it not common knowledge in those days that you could catch syphilis just by drinking from a glass?

It was not pleasant, but I learned what I had to learn. After all, I had chosen the profession of my own free will.

I would not have asked to change post for anything in the world. It was my superiors who did that, more out of a concern for getting their money's worth, I suppose, than out of consideration for me.

I was assigned to the railway stations. To be more precise, I was assigned to a certain dark and sinister building known as the Gare du Nord.

As with the department stores, there was the advantage that you were sheltered from the rain. Not from the cold and wind, because I doubt that there is a draughtier place anywhere in the world than the concourse of a railway station, the concourse of the Gare du Nord for example, and, for months, as far as colds went, I gave old Lagrume a run for his money.

I would not like anyone to think that I am complaining, or that I am deliberately depicting the dark side of things as an act of revenge.

I was perfectly happy. I had been happy tramping the streets, and no less happy when I was keeping an eye out for so-called kleptomaniacs in the department stores.

Each time I had the impression I was going up a notch, learning a trade which seemed ever more complex with each passing day.

Whenever I see the Gare de l'Est, I can never help feeling sad, because it conjures up the image of men going off to war. The Gare de Lyon, on the other hand, like the Gare Montparnasse, makes me think of holidays.

The Gare du Nord, the coldest and busiest of all, mainly evokes for me a bitter struggle for daily bread. Is it because it leads to the regions of mines and factories?

In the morning, the first night trains from Belgium and Germany generally contain a few smugglers, a few traffickers, their faces as hard as the daylight seen through the windows.

They are not always small fry. Some are professionals in international trafficking, with their agents, their men of straw and their henchmen, people who play for high stakes and are ready to defend themselves by every means possible.

No sooner has that crowd dispersed than it is the turn of the suburban trains, coming not from pleasant villages like those in the west or the south, but from dark, unhealthy conurbations.

But those who, for whatever reason, are attempting to flee leave in the opposite direction, towards Belgium, the nearest border.

Hundreds of people wait in a grey murk smelling of smoke and sweat, or bustle about, running from ticket office to left-luggage, checking the arrivals and departures boards, eating and drinking, surrounded by children, dogs and suitcases, and almost always they are people who have not slept enough, who are made irritable by the fear of being late, or sometimes simply the fear of what the future will bring in whichever place they are going.

I spent hours every day watching them, searching among those faces for a face that was more inscrutable, eyes that were more vacant, the eyes of a man or woman risking all on one last chance.

The train is there, waiting to leave in a few minutes. They just have to walk a hundred metres and hold out the ticket they are clutching. The hands on the huge yellow face of the clock advance jerkily.

Double or quits! A matter of freedom or prison. Or worse.

Me with a photograph in my wallet, or a description, sometimes only a technical description of an ear.

Sometimes we spot each other at the same moment, and our eyes meet. Almost always, the man realizes immediately.

What happens next depends on his character, the risk he is running, his nerves, even some small material detail, a door that is open or closed, a trunk that just happens to be between us.

Some try to get away, and there is a desperate chase through groups that protest or move aside, through stationary carriages, the tracks, the points.

I have known two, including one very young man, who, at an interval of three months, did an identical thing.

They both plunged their hands in their pockets as if to get a cigarette. And a moment later, right there in the middle of the crowd, their eyes fixed on me, they shot themselves in the head.

They did not bear me any grudge, any more than I bore them a grudge.

We were each doing our job.

They had lost the game, that was all, and now they bowed out.

I had also lost, because my role was to catch them alive and bring them to justice.

I have seen thousands of trains leave. I have seen thousands of others arrive, with the same crush each time, the long line of people rushing to one thing or another.

For me, as for my colleagues, it has become a habit. Even when I am not on duty, even when, by some miracle, my wife and I are setting off on holiday, my eyes move from face to face, and it is quite rare that they do not eventually linger on someone who is afraid, however hard he may be trying to hide it.

'Aren't you coming? What's the matter?'

Not until we are settled in our compartment – no, not until the train has left – is my wife sure that the holiday will really happen.

'What are you looking at? You're not on duty!'

I have sometimes followed her with a sigh, turning my head one last time – always regretfully – to a mysterious face disappearing into the crowd.

And I do not think it is solely out of professional concern, nor out of a love of justice.

I repeat: it is a game that is being played, a game that has no end. Once it has started, it is quite difficult, if not impossible, to leave it.

The proof of that is that those of us who finally retire, often reluctantly, almost always end up starting a private detective agency.

Of course that is nothing but a stopgap, and I do not know a single officer who, after complaining for thirty years about the miseries of a policeman's life, is not ready to go back on duty, even unpaid.

I have retained a sinister memory of the Gare du Nord. For some reason I always see it filled with the damp, sticky fog of early morning, with its crowds of people barely awake walking towards either the platforms or Rue de Maubeuge.

The specimens of humanity I have met there are among the most desperate, and some arrests I have made there have left me rather with a feeling of remorse than one of professional satisfaction.

If I had to choose, though, I would rather take up my position tomorrow at the entrance to the platforms than set off from a grander station for some sunny corner of the Riviera.

6.

Stairs, stairs and more stairs!

From time to time, almost always at times of political unrest, there are disturbances in the streets, which are no longer simply a manifestation of popular discontent. It is as if at a certain moment a breach occurs, invisible floodgates are opened, and all of a sudden people appear in rich neighbourhoods whose existence is generally ignored there, people who seem to have come straight from some medieval den of iniquity, and who are watched as they pass beneath the windows as if they were rogues and cut-throats from the remote past.

What surprised me the most, when this phenomenon occurred with such violence following the riots of 6 February, was the astonishment expressed the following day by most of the press.

This invasion of the centre of Paris for several hours, not by demonstrators, but by individuals who were all skin and bone, spread as much terror as a pack of wolves, and alarmed people who, by profession, have almost as great a knowledge of the underbelly of a large city as we do.

Paris really was afraid that time. But the very next day, once order had been restored, Paris forgot that this populace had not been wiped out, but had simply gone to ground again.

After all, the police are around to keep them there, aren't they?

Is it generally known that there is a squad dealing exclusively with the roughly two to three hundred thousand North Africans, Portuguese and Romanians living, or rather, subsisting, in the slums of the twentieth arrondissement, barely knowing our language or not knowing it at all, obeying other laws, other instincts than ours?

At Quai des Orfèvres, we have maps on which various pockets are marked with coloured pencils: the Jews in Rue des Rosiers, the Italians around the Hôtel de Ville, the Russians in the Ternes and Denfert-Rochereau . . .

Many ask nothing but to assimilate, and they do not cause us any difficulties. But there are some who, in groups or as individuals, deliberately keep themselves on the margins and lead their own mysterious lives in the midst of a crowd that does not notice them.

It is almost always right-thinking people, with their carefully camouflaged little deceptions and vices, who ask me, with that slight trembling of the lips I know so well:

'Don't you sometimes feel disgusted?'

They are not talking about any one thing in particular, but those we deal with as a whole. What they would really like is for us to tell them some nice dirty secrets, some unheard-of vices, a whole world of squalor they can wax indignant over, while secretly revelling in it.

It is people like that who love to use the word *slums*.

'The things you must see down there in the slums!'

I prefer not to answer them. I look at them in a certain way, without any expression on my face, and I assume they understand what that means, because they usually look embarrassed and do not insist.

I learned a lot on the beat. I learned things in the fairs and in the department stores, everywhere where crowds were gathered.

I have spoken about my experiences at the Gare du Nord.

But it was probably in the hotels squad that I gained most knowledge of the kinds of people who scare those from the nice neighbourhoods whenever the floodgates are opened.

The hobnailed boots were not necessary here, because I did not have to walk kilometres of pavement. I circulated, so to speak, at a higher level.

Every day, I would collect forms from dozens, hundreds of hotels, most of them rooming houses, where it was rare to find a lift and you had to climb six or seven floors, up stifling stairwells, where an acrid smell of poverty took you by the throat.

The grand hotels with their revolving doors flanked by uniformed valets also have their dramas and their secrets, into which the police are constantly sticking their noses.

But it is above all in the thousands of hotels with unknown names, barely noticed from the outside, that a floating population goes to ground, a population difficult to grab hold of elsewhere and seldom with their papers in order.

We would go in pairs. Sometimes, in dangerous neighbourhoods, there were more of us. We would choose an hour when most people were in bed, not long after the middle of the night.

Then a kind of nightmare would begin. Some details were always the same: the night porter or the owner asleep behind his desk, reluctantly waking up and trying to cover himself in advance.

'You know we've never had any problems here . . .'

In the old days, the names were written in registers. Later, with the introduction of compulsory identity cards, there were forms to fill in.

One of us would remain downstairs. The other would go up. Sometimes, in spite of all our precautions, we would hear the house come alive like a beehive, frantic comings and goings in the rooms, furtive footsteps on the stairs.

We would sometimes find an empty room, the bed still warm, and the skylight looking out over the roofs open.

Usually, we were able to reach the top floor without alarming the guests and we would knock at the first door, to be answered with groans and questions in a language that was almost always foreign.

'Police!'

They all understand that word. And people in night-shirts, others stark naked, men and women and children, moved about in the bad light, in the bad smell, unfastened incredible trunks looking for passports hidden under all their things.

You have to have seen the anxiety in those eyes, those sleepwalking gestures, and that quality of humility one finds only in the uprooted. Shall I call it a proud humility?

They did not hate us. We were the masters. We had – or they believed we had – the most terrible of all powers: the power to send them back across the border.

For some, the fact that they were here represented years of scheming or patience. They had reached the promised land. They had papers, true or false.

And as they held them out to us, always afraid we would put them in our pockets, they would try instinctively to cajole us with a smile, finding a few words of French to stammer:

'M'sieu Inspector Sir . . .'

The women rarely made any attempt at modesty, and sometimes there was a look in their eyes, a hesitant gesture towards the unmade bed. Weren't we tempted? Wouldn't that give us pleasure?

And yet all these people were proud, with a special kind of pride I find hard to describe. The pride of animals?

Sure enough, they were rather like animals in cages as they looked at us, uncertain if we were going to hit them or encourage them.

Sometimes you would see one who would brandish his papers in a kind of panic and start speaking volubly in his language, gesticulating, calling the others to his aid, making an effort to convince us that he was an honest man, that things were not as they seemed, that . . .

Some wept and others huddled in their corners, hostile, as if ready to pounce, but actually resigned.

An identity check. That is what the operation is called in official language. Those whose papers are unquestionably in order are left in their rooms, and you hear them locking their doors with a sigh of relief.

The others . . .

'Come downstairs!'

When they do not understand, you have to add a gesture. They get dressed, talking to themselves. They have no idea what to take with them. Sometimes, as soon as our backs are turned, they look for their money in some hiding place and stuff it in their pockets or under their shirts.

On the ground floor, they form a little group. Nobody speaks, each person is thinking only of his own case and the way he is going to plead it.

In the Saint-Antoine district, there are hotels where I have sometimes found seven or eight Poles in a single room, most of them sleeping on the floor.

Only one was mentioned in the register. Did the owner know? Did he get money for the extra sleepers? More than likely, but that is the kind of thing it is pointless to try and prove.

Of course, the others' papers were not in order. What did they do when they were forced to leave the shelter of their room early in the morning?

Without work permits, it was impossible for them to earn their living regularly. They were clearly not dying of starvation. Which meant they ate.

And there were, there still are thousands, tens of thousands in the same position.

If we find money in their pockets, hidden on top of a wardrobe, or, more often, in their shoes, we then have to find out how they got it, and that is the most exhausting kind of interrogation.

Even when they understand French, they pretend not to, looking you in the eyes with an air of goodwill, tirelessly repeating their protestations of innocence.

It is pointless to question the others about them. They will not betray each other. They will all tell the same story.

But on average, sixty-five per cent of crimes committed in the Paris region are committed by foreigners.

Stairs, stairs and more stairs. Not only at night, but by day, and everywhere girls, some professional prostitutes, others not. Some are so young and beautiful, you wonder why they have come all the way from their countries.

I knew one, a Polish girl, who shared a hotel room in Rue Saint-Antoine with five men and told them which places to rob. She would reward those who succeeded in her own way, while the others champed at the bit in the room, then usually threw themselves angrily on the exhausted winner.

Two of them were enormous, powerful brutes, but she was not afraid of them, she kept them at a respectful distance with a smile or a frown. When I interrogated them in my own office, I saw her calmly slap one of the giants after something he had said in their language.

'You must have seen all sorts!'

And indeed, you see men and women, all sorts of men and women, in all kinds of unlikely situations, at all levels of the scale. You see them, you record them, and you try to understand.

Not to understand some kind of human mystery. That may be the romantic idea I most firmly, even angrily, object to. That is one of the reasons for this book: to correct that kind of misconception.

Simenon has tried to explain it, I admit that. And yet I have been embarrassed to see myself smile in a certain way in his books, express certain attitudes I have never had, attitudes that would have made my colleagues shrug.

The person who has felt it most keenly is most probably my wife. And yet when I get home from work, she never questions me, whatever case I am dealing with.

For my part, I never make what are called confidences.

I sit down at the table like any other civil servant coming back from his office. I may then, in a few words, as if to myself, talk about an encounter, an interrogation, the man or woman I have been investigating.

If she asks me a question, it is almost always a technical one.

'In what district?'

Or else:

'How old?'

Or even:

'How long has she been in France?'

Because, over time, these details have become as revealing to her as they are to us.

She does not ask me about any of the sordid or pitiful aspects.

God knows it is not indifference on her part!

'Did his wife go to see him in the cells?'

'Yes, this morning.'

'Did she bring the child with her?'

She is particularly interested, for reasons on which I do not have to insist, in those who have children, and it would be a mistake to think that illegals, gangsters or criminals do not have any.

We took one in once, a little girl whose mother I had sent to prison for the rest of her days, but we knew that the father would come and collect her as soon as he returned to normal.

She still comes to see us. She is a young woman now, and my wife is quite proud to take her shopping in the afternoon.

What I am trying to emphasize is that in our behaviour towards those we deal with, there is neither sentimentality nor harshness, neither hatred nor pity in the usual sense of the word.

We handle human beings. We observe their behaviour. We record facts, try to establish others.

Our knowledge is, in a way, technical.

When I was a young man and would visit a shady hotel, entering each cell-like room from the cellar to the attic, surprising people in their sleep, in all their crude intimacy, examining their papers with a magnifying glass, I could almost have said what would become of each of them.

Firstly, some faces were already familiar to me, because Paris is not so large that, within a given milieu, you do not constantly meet the same individuals.

Secondly, some cases were reproduced almost identically, the same causes bringing about the same results.

The unfortunate who has come from central Europe, who has saved for months, perhaps years, to afford to buy a false passport from a clandestine agency in his country, and who thought it was all over when he crossed the border without any problems, will inevitably fall into our hands within six months or a year at most.

Better still: we can predict his every move from the border, know exactly in which area, in which restaurant, in which hotel, he will end up.

We know from whom he will try to acquire the indispensable work permit, whether genuine or fake. We just have to go and pick him up from the queues that form every morning outside the big factories in Javel.

Why get angry or resentful when he finishes up exactly where he was bound to finish up?

It is the same with the fresh-faced young parlour maid we see dancing for the first time in some *bal musette*. Should we tell her to go home to her employers and avoid her flashily dressed companion from now on?

It would be pointless. She will go back to him. We will see her in other *bal musettes*, then, one fine evening, standing in the doorway of a hotel around Les Halles or the Bastille.

Every year, ten thousand pass that way on average, ten thousand who leave their villages and arrive in Paris as domestic servants, and who only take a few months, or even a few weeks, to go downhill.

Is it so different when a young man of eighteen or twenty, who has been working in a factory, starts dressing and behaving in a particular way, propping up the counters of particular bars?

We will soon see him in a new suit, with artificial silk socks and tie.

He will end up with us, too, looking shifty or contrite, after an attempted burglary or an armed robbery, unless he signed on to join the legion of car thieves.

Some signs are unmistakable, and when all is said and done it is those signs we learned to recognize when we were made to go from squad to squad, to tramp kilometres of pavement, to climb floor after floor, to go into every kind of slum and through every kind of crowd.

That is why the nickname 'Hobnailed Boots' has never bothered us. Quite the contrary.

By the age of forty, there are few of us at Quai des Orfèvres who are not familiar, for example, with all the pickpockets. We even know where to find them on such and such a day, on the occasion of such a ceremony or such a gala.

Just as we know, for example, that a jewel robbery will soon be taking place, because a specialist whom we have seldom caught red-handed is starting to get to the end of his tether. He has left his hotel on Boulevard Haussmann for a more modest hotel near Place de la République. For the past fortnight, he has not paid his bills. The woman he lives with is starting to kick up a fuss and has not been able to afford any new hats for a long time.

We cannot follow his every step: there will never be enough police officers to tail all suspects. But we keep him on a short leash. The beat officers are alerted to keep a particular eye on jewellers' shops. We know how he operates.

It does not always work. That would be too good to be true. But we do sometimes catch him in the act. And sometimes this is after a discreet conversation with his companion, to whom we make it clear that her future would be less problematic if she kept us informed.

There is a lot written in the newspapers about gangsters settling scores in Montmartre or around Rue Fontaine, because gunshots in the night always thrill the public.

But it is these cases that give us the fewest problems at the Quai.

We know the rival gangs, their interests, the points of contention between them. We also know their hatreds and their personal resentments.

One crime leads to another. Was Luciano shot down in a bar in Rue de Douai? The Corsicans will inevitably retaliate within a relatively short time. And almost always, one of them will tip us off.

'Someone's planning to take down Flatfoot Dédé. He knows it and always has two bodyguards with him when he goes out.'

The day Dédé is shot down in his turn, there are nine chances out of ten that a more or less mysterious telephone call will bring us up to date with the story in all its details.

'One less to worry about!'

We arrest the culprits all the same, but it does not really matter, because these people only kill each other, for reasons that are theirs alone, according to a code they apply to the letter.

That is what Simenon was referring to when, in the course of our first conversation, he declared so categorically:

'I'm not interested in the crimes of professional criminals.'

What he did not yet know, but has learned since, is that there are very few other crimes.

I am not talking about crimes of passion, which for the most part are lacking in mystery, being merely the logical outcome of an acute crisis between two or more individuals.

Nor am I talking about a knife fight on a Saturday or Sunday night between two drunks in some area.

Apart from these accidents, the most common crimes are of two kinds:

The murder of some solitary old woman by one or several young thugs, and the murder of a prostitute on a stretch of waste ground.

For the former, it is extremely rare for the culprit to get away. Almost always, he is a young man, one of those I spoke about earlier, who stopped working in a factory a few months ago and is eager to play the tough guy.

He homes in on a tobacconist's, a haberdasher's, or some other little business in a deserted street.

Sometimes he buys a revolver. Other times, he makes do with a hammer or a spanner.

He almost always knows the victim, and in at least one case out of ten the victim was good to him in the past.

He does not intend to kill. He puts a scarf over his face in order not to be recognized.

The handkerchief slips, or else the old woman starts screaming.

He shoots her, if he has a gun, or hits her. If he shoots, he empties the whole barrel, which is a sign of panic. If he hits her, he does so ten, twenty times – what is called a savage attack, although actually it is because he is driven mad with fear.

It may surprise you to hear that when we have him in front of us, crushed but still trying to brazen it out, we simply say to him, 'You fool!'

It is rare for such young men not to pay with their lives. The least they get is twenty years, when they are lucky enough to get a leading lawyer interested in their case.

As for the killers of prostitutes, it is a miracle when we get our hands on them. Those are the longest, the most discouraging, and also the most sickening investigations I know.

It begins with a sack fished out of the Seine somewhere by a sailor with his boat hook. In it, there is almost always a mutilated body. The head is missing, or an arm, or the legs.

Often, weeks pass before any identification is possible. Generally, it is a prostitute of a certain age, the kind who no longer take their clients to a hotel or to their room, but make do with a doorway or the shelter of a fence.

People have stopped seeing her around the neighbourhood, a neighbourhood that is wrapped in mystery and silent shadows.

The women who know her do not want to have any dealings with us. When they are questioned, they just stare straight ahead of them.

Eventually, through patient work, we end up with the names of some of her regular clients, isolated, solitary, ageless men who leave little behind but a vague memory.

Was she killed for her money? Unlikely, given how little she had!

Did one of those old men suddenly go mad, or was it someone from elsewhere, from another neighbourhood, one of those madmen who, at regular intervals, feel the crisis coming, know exactly what they will do and, with incredible lucidity, take the kinds of precautions of which other criminals are incapable?

We do not even know how many of them there are. Every capital has its own. Once they have done their work, they plunge back into anonymity for an indefinite length of time.

They may be respectable people, family men, model employees.

What exactly they look like, nobody knows, and when by chance one of them is caught, it is almost always impossible to gain a satisfactory conviction.

We have fairly accurate statistics for all these kinds of crimes.

With one exception.

Poisoning.

And all approximations would inevitably be false, either too large or too small.

Every three to six months, in Paris or in the provinces, especially in the provinces, in a small town or in the countryside, a doctor happens, quite by chance, to examine a dead person more closely and is struck by certain features.

I say 'by chance', because it is usually one of his patients, someone who has been sick for a long time. This person has died suddenly in his bed, surrounded by his family, who show all the traditional signs of grief.

The relatives will not hear of an autopsy. The doctor only decides to do one if his suspicions are strong enough.

Alternatively, weeks after a funeral, the police receive an anonymous letter supplying details that seem unbelievable at first sight.

I am insisting in order to show all the conditions that have to come together for an investigation of this kind to be launched. The bureaucratic formalities are complicated.

Most of the time, it is a farmer's wife who has been waiting years for her husband to die so that she can set up home with the servant and could wait no longer.

She has given nature a helping hand, as some rather crudely put it.

Sometimes, although this is rarer, it is a man getting rid of a sick wife who has become a dead weight in the house.

They are discovered by chance. But in how many other cases does chance not intervene? We have no idea. We can merely surmise. There are some, both in our house and the one in Rue des Saussaies, who think that of all crimes, especially those that go unpunished, this is the most frequent.

The others, those that interest novelists and so-called psychologists, are so uncommon that they take up only an insignificant part of our activities.

And yet it is those which the public knows best. It is those cases that Simenon has mostly written about and will, I assume, continue to write about.

I mean crimes that are suddenly committed in places where you would least expect them, and that are something like the end-product of a long-hidden period of fermentation.

An ordinary street, clean and cosy, in Paris or elsewhere. People who have a comfortable house, a family life, a respectable profession.

We have never had to cross their threshold before. Often it is a place where we would not normally be admitted, where we would stick out like a sore thumb and feel awkward to say the least.

And yet someone has died violently, and here we are knocking at the door, to be confronted by inscrutable faces, a family in which each member seems to have his secret.

Here, the experience acquired during years on the beat, at the railway stations, in the hotels squad, does not apply. Nor is there the kind of instinctive respect that poor people show towards authority, towards the police.

Nobody is afraid of being escorted to the border. Nor will anybody be taken to an office at the Quai to be subjected to hours of questioning.

Those we have in front of us are the same right-thinking people who would have asked us in other circumstances:

'Don't you sometimes feel disgusted?'

It is in a place like this that we do feel disgusted. Not immediately. Not always. Because the task is long and hazardous.

Provided there isn't a telephone call from a minister, a deputy or some other important figure trying to take us off the case.

There is a whole veneer of respectability that has to be cracked little by little, there are family secrets, more or less repugnant, which everyone gets together to hide from us and which it is essential to bring into the light of day, unconcerned about protests or threats.

Sometimes, there are five, six, or more people telling the same lies, while at the same time trying insidiously to incriminate the others.

Simenon likes to describe me as being heavy and grouchy, ill at ease in my skin, looking at people in a shifty way, barking my questions bad-temperedly.

It is in such cases that he has seen me like that, faced with what could be called amateur crimes which you *always* end up discovering are crimes of self-interest.

Not crimes of money. I am not talking about crimes committed out of a pressing need for money, as with those young thugs who murder old ladies.

No, behind those façades there are more complicated long-term interests, combined with concerns for respectability. Often, it all goes back years, through whole lifetimes of trickery and deception.

When people are finally forced to confess, there is a foul stream of revelations, and above all, almost always, an absolute terror of the consequences.

'Our family can't possibly be dragged through the mud, can it? We have to find a solution.'

That happens, I regret to say. There are those who should only have left my office for a cell in the Santé, but who have simply dropped out of sight, because there are spheres of influence against which a police inspector, even a detective chief inspector, is powerless.

'Don't you sometimes feel disgusted?'

I never felt disgusted when, as an inspector in the hotels squad, I spent my days or nights climbing the stairs of filthy, overcrowded rooming houses, where each door opened on to a world of misery and tragedy.

Nor does the word disgust apply to my reactions to those thousands of professional criminals of all kinds I have had to deal with.

They played their game and lost. Almost all of them were determined to show that they were good players, and some, once sentenced, would even ask me to go and see them in prison, where we chatted like friends.

I could mention several who asked me to be present at their execution, who wanted me to be the last person they saw before they died.

'I'll be fine, you'll see!'

They did their best. They did not always succeed. I carried their last letters away with me in my pocket and made sure I delivered each with a little note from me.

When I got home, my wife only had to look at me without asking any questions to know how things had gone.

As for the others, on whom I prefer not to linger, she also knew the meaning of certain bad moods, of a certain way of sitting down at the table when I got home in the evening and shovelling food on to my plate, and she would not insist.

Which is perfect proof that she was not intended for someone in the Highways Department!

7.

*About a morning as triumphant as a bugle call and a young man
who was no longer thin but not yet completely fat*

I can still recall the taste, the colour of the sun that morning. It was in March. Spring had come early. I was already in the habit of walking whenever I could from Boulevard Richard-Lenoir to Quai des Orfèvres.

I had no work to do outside that day, only files to sort in the offices of the hotels squad – probably the darkest offices in the whole of the Palais de Justice, located on the ground floor, with a little door, which I had left open, leading to the courtyard.

I kept as close to that door as my work allowed. I remember the sun cutting the courtyard exactly in two, including a waiting Black Maria. Its two horses tapped their hooves on the cobbles from time to time, and behind them there was a fine heap of golden dung, steaming in the still chilly air.

For some reason, the courtyard reminded me of certain playtimes at school, at that same time of year, when the air suddenly starts to have a scent and your skin, when you have been running, smells like the spring.

I was alone in the office. The telephone rang.

'Will you tell Maigret that the chief wants him?'

The voice of the office boy from upstairs – not a boy any more, since he had spent nearly fifty years in the same post.

'This is Maigret.'

'Then come up.'

Even the always dusty main staircase seemed a cheerful place, with slanting rays of sunlight as if in a church. The morning report had just finished. Two chief inspectors were still in conversation, their files under their arms, outside the chief's door, on which I was about to knock.

Once inside the office, I could smell the pipes and cigarettes of those who had just left it. A window was open behind Xavier Guichard, who had plumes of sunlight in his silky white hair.

He did not hold out his hand. He almost never did so in the office. All the same, we had become friends or, to be more precise, he was kind enough to honour my wife and me with his friendship. The first time, he had invited me alone to his apartment on Boulevard Saint-Germain. Not the rich, snobbish part of the boulevard. On the contrary, he lived just opposite Place Maubert, in a large new apartment block surrounded by rickety houses and seedy hotels.

The second time, I had gone there with my wife. The two of them had immediately got on well.

He certainly felt affection for her, and for me, and yet he often hurt us without meaning to.

In the beginning, as soon as he saw Louise he would look at her figure insistently and, if we appeared not to understand, he would cough and say, 'Don't forget I want to be the godfather.'

He was a confirmed bachelor. Apart from his brother, who was head of the municipal police, he had no family in Paris.

'Don't keep me waiting too long . . .'

Years had passed, and he still had not caught on. I remember that when he had announced my first pay rise to me, he had added, 'Maybe now you can give me a godson.'

He never understood why we blushed, why my wife lowered her eyes while I reached out my hand to console her.

That morning, standing against the light, he seemed very grave. He did not ask me to sit, and I felt embarrassed by the insistence with which he looked me up and down, like an adjutant in the army examining a recruit.

'You know you're putting on weight, Maigret?'

I was thirty. I had gradually stopped being thin, my shoulders had grown broader, my chest had swelled, but I had not yet reached my true build.

It was obvious, though. I must have looked flabby at the time, with something of the baby about me. I was struck by it myself whenever I passed a shop window and threw an anxious glance at my reflection.

It was too much or too little, and no suit would fit me.

'Yes, I think I'm putting on weight.'

I almost felt like apologizing. I had not yet grasped that he was amusing himself, as he liked to do.

'I think I should give you a change of department.'

There were two squads I had not yet been part of, the gambling section and the financial squad, and the latter was my nightmare, just as the end-of-year trigonometry exam had long been my nightmare at school.

'How old are you?'

'Thirty.'

'A good age! It's perfect. Young Lesueur will take your place in hotels, as of today, and you'll make yourself available to Chief Inspector Guillaume.'

He had deliberately said it in a half-hearted tone, as if it were unimportant, knowing that my heart would leap in my chest. Standing in front of him, I heard something like a fanfare of trumpets in my ears.

All at once, on a morning that seemed to have been chosen deliberately – and I cannot say for sure that Guichard did not do so – the great dream of my life had come true.

I was finally joining the Special Squad.

A quarter of an hour later, I moved upstairs, with my old office jacket, my soap, my towel, my pencils and a few papers.

There were five or six men in the large room reserved for inspectors of the homicide squad, and before sending for me, Chief Inspector Guillaume let me settle in, like a new pupil.

'Shall we have a drink?'

I was hardly going to say no. At midday, I proudly took my new colleagues to the Brasserie Dauphine.

I had often seen them there, at another table to the one I occupied with my former colleagues, and we would look at them with the envious respect granted, at school, to the final-year pupils, who are as tall as the teachers and are treated by them almost as equals.

The comparison was an accurate one, because Guillaume was with us, and we were joined by the chief inspector from the police intelligence service.

'What will you have?' I asked.

In our corner, we had been in the habit of drinking beer, or very occasionally an aperitif. Obviously, the same could not apply at this table.

Someone said, 'Mandarin-curaçao.'

'Mandarins all round?'

As nobody objected, I ordered mandarins – I do not remember how many. It was the first time I had tasted it. In the intoxication of victory, it struck me as barely alcoholic.

'Another round?'

If now was not a time to be generous, when would be? We had a third round, then a fourth. My new chief also stood us a round.

The city was full of sunlight. The streets were bathed in it. The women in their bright dresses were an enchantment. I weaved my way between the pedestrians. I looked at myself in the shop windows and did not think I was as fat as all that.

I ran. I flew. I leaped for joy. I was still at the foot of the stairs when I started the speech I had prepared for my wife.

And on the last flight of stairs, I fell headlong. I did not have time to pick myself up before our door opened: Louise must have been worried by my lateness.

'Did you hurt yourself?'

The funny thing is that from the moment I got back on my feet, I knew I was dead drunk and it was a complete surprise to me. The stairs were spinning around me. My wife was just a blurred figure. She seemed to have at least two mouths and three or four eyes.

Believe it or not, it was the first time it had ever happened in my life, and I felt so humiliated that I did not dare look at her. I slipped into the apartment like a guilty person, completely forgetting the words of triumph I had so carefully prepared.

'I think . . . I think I'm a little drunk . . .'

My nose felt blocked. The table was laid, with our two place settings facing each other by the open window. I had promised myself I would take her out for lunch, but I no longer dared suggest it.

It was in an almost lugubrious voice that I said, 'It's happened.'

'What's happened?'

Maybe she was expecting me to tell her that I had been thrown out of the police force!

'I've been moved.'

'Moved to what?'

Apparently I had big tears in my eyes, of vexation, but doubtless also of joy, as I blurted out, 'The Special Squad.'

'Sit down. I'll make you a cup of very black coffee.'

She tried to put me to bed, but I was hardly going to abandon my new post on the first day. I do not know how many cups of strong coffee I drank. In spite of Louise's insistence, I could not swallow anything solid. I took a shower.

At two o'clock, when I set off back to Quai des Orfèvres, my complexion was unusually pink, and my eyes were shining. I felt slack, my head empty.

I went and took my seat in my corner and spoke as little as possible, because I knew my voice was unsteady and I would probably mix up the syllables.

The next day, as if to put me to the test, they gave me my first arrest. It was in a rooming house in Rue du Roi-de-Sicile. The man had already been tailed for five days. He had several murders to his name. He was a foreigner, a Czech, if I remember correctly, very well-built, always armed, always on the alert.

The problem was to immobilize him before he had time to defend himself, because he was the kind of person who would shoot into the crowd and kill as many people as possible before letting himself be killed.

He knew that he had reached the end of the road, that the police were on his trail and were about to pounce.

Out on the streets, he always made sure he was surrounded by crowds, aware that we could not take any risks.

I was assigned to Inspector Dufour, who had been dealing with him for several days and knew all his comings and goings.

It was also the first time I disguised myself. Going to that wretched rooming house dressed as we usually were would have thrown everyone into a panic, and our man might have taken advantage of it to get away.

Dufour and I dressed in old rags and, to make it even more convincing, did not shave for forty-eight hours.

A young inspector who specialized in locks had got into the building and made us an excellent copy of the door key.

We took another room on the same landing, before the Czech came back to sleep. It was just after eleven when a signal from outside told us he was coming up the stairs.

The tactic we followed was not mine, but Dufour's. After all, he had been around a lot longer than me.

Not far from us, the man was locking himself in and lying down fully clothed on his bed, probably with at least one loaded gun within reach.

We did not sleep. We waited for dawn. If I am asked why, I will say what my colleague said when, in my impatience to get moving, I asked him the same question.

The murderer's first reflex, on hearing us, would no doubt have been to smash the gas lamp in his room. We would have found ourselves in the dark, thus giving him an advantage over us.

'A man always puts up less resistance early in the morning,' Dufour asserted: something I was able subsequently to verify.

We slipped out into the corridor. Everyone was asleep around us. With infinite care, Dufour turned the key in the lock.

As I was taller and heavier, it was up to me to rush in first, and I did so, in one bound, and found myself lying on top of the man in the bed, grabbing him by whatever I could grab.

I do not know how long the struggle lasted, but it seemed endless. I felt us rolling to the ground. I saw his rage-filled face close to mine. I particularly remember his big, dazzling white teeth. A hand grabbed my ear and tried to tear it off.

I was not aware of what my colleague was doing, but I saw an expression of pain and fury on my opponent's features and felt him gradually relax his grip. When I was able to turn, I saw Inspector Dufour sitting cross-legged on the floor with one of the man's feet in his hands, and could have sworn he had already twisted it at least twice.

'Handcuffs!' he ordered.

I had already put handcuffs on less dangerous individuals, on recalcitrant prostitutes. This was the first time I had carried out such a violent arrest and the sound of the handcuffs put an end to a fight that could have gone badly.

When people talk about a policeman's nose, his sixth sense, his intuition, I always feel like retorting, 'What about your cobbler's intuition, or your pastry maker's?'

Both have had years of apprenticeship. Each knows his trade, and everything that pertains to his trade.

It is no different with someone from Quai des Orfèvres. And that is why all the stories I have read, including those of my friend Simenon, are inaccurate to a greater or lesser degree.

We are in our office, writing reports. Because this too, as is all too often forgotten, is part of the profession. I would even say that we spend much more time dealing with paperwork about cases than working on the cases themselves.

Someone comes in and announces that a nervous-looking middle-aged man is in the waiting room. He says he wants to speak to the commissioner immediately. Needless to say, the commissioner does not have time to see all the people who show up and demand to speak to him personally, because as far as they are concerned their little problem is the only one that matters.

There is a sentence used so often it has become a refrain, which the office boy recites like a litany: 'It's a matter of life and death.'

'Will you see him, Maigret?'

There is a little office next to the inspectors' office for that kind of interview.

'Please take a seat. Cigarette?'

Most of the time, even though the visitor has not yet had time to tell us his profession, his social status, we have already guessed it.

'It's a very delicate, very personal matter.'

A bank clerk, or an insurance agent, a man with a quiet, calm life.

'Your daughter?'

It is either his son or his daughter or his wife. And we can predict what he is going to tell us, practically word for word. No, his son has not taken money from his boss's till. And his wife has not run away with a young man.

No, this is all about his daughter, a young girl who has had the best upbringing, who has never done anything untoward. She has not been seeing anyone, has always lived at home and helped her mother with the housework.

Her friends are as dependable as she is. She has almost never gone out alone.

All the same, she has disappeared, taking some of her things with her.

What can you say in reply? That every month six hundred people disappear in Paris, and only about two thirds of them are ever found again?

'Is your daughter very pretty?'

He has brought several photographs, convinced they will be useful in the search. It is unfortunate if she is pretty, because then the chances of finding her decrease. If she is ugly, on the other hand, she will probably be back in a few days or a few weeks.

'Count on us. We'll do all we can.'

'When?'

'Immediately.'

He will telephone us every day, twice a day, and there is nothing to tell him, except that we have not yet had time to look for the girl.

Almost always, a brief inquiry indicates that a young man living in the same building, or the grocer's assistant, or the brother of one of her girlfriends, has disappeared on the same day as she did.

We cannot search Paris and France with a fine-tooth comb for a runaway girl, and the following week her photograph will simply be added to the collection of photographs that are sent to police stations, to the different police departments and the borders.

Eleven o'clock at night. A phone call from the police emergency centre opposite, in the buildings of the municipal police, where all calls are centralized and are shown on a luminous board that takes up a whole wall.

The station at Pont-de-Flandre has just been informed that things are turning nasty in a bar in Rue de Crimée.

That means crossing the whole of Paris. Today, the Police Judiciaire has several cars at its disposal, but in the old days, we had to take a carriage or, later, a taxi, and we were not always sure we would be reimbursed.

The bar is on the corner of the street. It is still open. The window has been smashed. There are people outside, keeping a cautious distance, because around here it is better not to be noticed by the police.

Uniformed officers are already there, along with an ambulance, and sometimes the local chief inspector or his secretary.

On the floor, amid the sawdust and spittle, lies a man, bent double, one hand on his chest. Blood has trickled onto the floor and formed a pool.

'Dead!'

Beside him, on the floor, is the small case he was holding in his hand when he fell. It has come open, and pornographic postcards have spilled out.

The owner is anxious to show himself in a good light.

'Everything was calm, as it always is. This is a quiet place.'

'Have you seen him before?'

'Never.'

That was to be expected. He probably knows him like the back of his hand, but he will claim to the end that this was the first time the man had ever come into his bar.

'What happened?'

The dead man is nondescript, middle-aged, or rather, ageless. His clothes are old and not very clean, and his shirt collar is black with grime.

No point looking for a family, an apartment. He must have lived from day to day in low-class rooming houses, from where he set off to ply his trade around the Tuileries and the Palais-Royal.

'There were three or four customers . . .'

No point either in asking where they are. They have run away and will not be back to make statements.

'Do you know them?'

'Vaguely. Just by sight.'

My God, we could give his answers for him!

'A stranger came in and sat down at the other end of the bar, just opposite that one.'

The bar is horseshoe-shaped, with upturned little glasses and a strong odour of cheap alcohol.

'They didn't say anything to each other. The first one looked scared. He put his hand in his pocket to pay . . .'

That was true, because there was no weapon on him.

'Without a word, the other man took out his gun and fired three times. He would probably have continued if his gun hadn't jammed. Then he calmly stuck his hat on his head and left.'

It is almost a signature. No need for intuition. The circles we have to look into are quite restricted.

There are not as many people as all that involved in the pornographic postcard trade. We know almost all of them. Periodically they pass through our hands, do a short term in prison and start again.

The shoes of the dead man – who has dirty feet and socks with holes in them – bear a trademark from Berlin.

He is a newcomer. Maybe they were trying to make it clear to him that he was not wanted in the area. Or maybe he was just an underling entrusted with the merchandise, who had kept the money for himself.

It will take three days, maybe four. It is unlikely to take more. The hotels squad will immediately be alerted, and by the following night they will have found out where the victim was living.

Equipped with his photograph, the vice squad will investigate on their side.

That afternoon, in the area of the Tuileries, we will arrest some of the individuals who ply the same trade, going up to passers-by with a mysterious air to offer their merchandise.

We will not be gentle with them. In the old days we were even less gentle than now.

'Have you ever seen this man?'

'No.'

'Are you sure you've never come across him?'

There is a very dark, very narrow little cell not much larger than a cupboard on the mezzanine, where we put people of that kind to help them to remember. It usually only takes a few hours before they start banging on the door.

'I think I've seen him.'

'What's his name?'

'I only know his first name: Otto.'

The tangle will gradually unwind, but unwind it will, like a solitary worm.

'He's a queer!'

Good! The fact that he is homosexual restricts the field even more.

'Did he hang around Rue de Bondy?'

It is almost inevitable. There is a little bar there that is frequented by practically all the homosexuals of a certain social level – the lowest. There is another one in Rue de Lappe, which has become a tourist attraction.

'Who did you see him with?'

That is pretty much it. All that remains, when we have the culprit within four walls, is to get him to make and sign a confession.

Not all cases are so simple. Some investigations take months. Some culprits are only arrested years later, sometimes by chance.

But in practically every case, the process is the same.

It is a question of *knowing*.

Knowing the milieu in which a crime is committed, knowing the lifestyle, habits, behaviour and reactions of the people involved in it, whether victims, perpetrators or mere witnesses.

Entering fully into their world, unperturbed, and speaking its language naturally.

This holds true if we are talking to a bar owner in La Villette or Porte d'Italie or Arabs in the slums, Poles or Italians, nightclub hostesses in Pigalle or young thugs in the Ternes.

It is equally true of the denizens of race-courses and gambling dens, safecrackers or jewel thieves.

That is why it is not a waste of time to pound the streets for years, or to climb the stairs of rooming houses, or to keep an eye open for shoplifters in department stores.

Like cobblers and pastry cooks, we do our apprenticeship, the only difference being that our apprenticeship may last our whole lives, because the number of circles we have to deal with is practically infinite.

The prostitutes, the pickpockets, the three-card-trick players, the conmen or the passers of false cheques recognize each other.

The same could be said of policemen after a certain number of years on the job. And it has nothing to do with hobnailed boots or moustaches.

I think it is the look in the eyes that gives the game away, a certain way of reacting – or rather, not reacting – to certain individuals, certain wretched situations, certain anomalies.

Whatever writers of novels may think, the policeman is above all a professional. He is a *civil servant*.

He is not there to solve clever puzzles or launch into exciting chases.

When he spends a night in the rain, watching a closed door or a lighted window, when he searches patiently for a familiar face on the terrace of a boulevard café, or prepares to give the third degree to a man pale-faced with terror, he is simply doing his job.

He is making a living, trying to earn, as honestly as possible, the money the government gives him at the end of every month as a reward for his services.

I know that when my wife reads these lines, she will shake her head, give me a reproachful look and perhaps say:

'You always exaggerate!'

She will probably add:

'You're going to give a false idea of yourself and your colleagues.'

She is right. It is possible I am exaggerating somewhat in the opposite direction. It is a reaction against the set ideas that have so often irritated me.

The number of times, after the appearance of a book by Simenon, my colleagues have watched me sardonically as I walked into my office!

I could read what they were thinking in their eyes: 'Ah, there goes God the Father!'

That is why I am so determined to use the words *civil servant*, which others consider reductive.

I have been a civil servant for almost my entire life. Thanks to Inspector Jacquemain, I became one when I was just out of my teens.

Just as my father, in his day, became an estate manager. With the same pride. With the same desire to learn everything about my trade and do my job as conscientiously as possible.

The difference between other civil servants and those on Quai des Orfèvres is that the latter hover between two worlds, so to speak.

In their clothes, their backgrounds, their apartments, their lifestyles, they are in no way different from other middle-class people, and share the same middle-class dream of a little house in the country.

And yet most of their time is spent in contact with the underside of that world, with the dregs, the scum, even the enemies of organized society.

I have often been struck by that. It is a strange situation, and one that has sometimes given me a sense of unease.

I live in a bourgeois apartment, where nice smells of simmering food await me, where everything is neat and tidy, clean and comfortable. Through my windows, I see only houses like mine, mothers walking their children on the boulevard, housewives off to do their shopping.

I belong to that environment, of course, to the so-called honest people.

But I know the others too, I know them well enough for a certain contact to have been established between them and me. The whores I pass on Place de la République know that I understand their language and the meaning of their gestures. The hooligan threading his way through the crowd, too.

And all the others I have met, whom I meet each day in the most intimate situations.

Is that enough to create a kind of bond?

It is not a question of excusing them, approving of them or absolving them. Nor is it a question of dressing them in some kind of halo, as was the fashion for a time.

It is a question of looking at them simply as realities, of looking at them with the eyes of knowledge.

Without curiosity, because curiosity is soon blunted.

Without hatred, of course.

Of looking at them, in short, as people who exist, people who, for the health of society, for the mainten-ance of the established order, need to be kept within certain boundaries, whether they like it or not, and punished when they go beyond those boundaries.

They know that perfectly well, and they do not bear us any grudge. As they so often put it:

'You're just doing your job.'

As for what they think of that job, I would rather not know.

Is it surprising that after twenty-five years, thirty years on the job, your gait is a little heavy, and your eyes heav-ier too, sometimes empty?

'Don't you sometimes feel disgusted?'

No! Why should I? It is probably thanks to this job that I have acquired a fairly staunch kind of optimism.

Paraphrasing a maxim from my catechism teacher, I am prepared to say: a little knowledge distances us from people, a lot of knowledge brings us closer.

It is because I have seen dirty deeds of all kinds that I have come to realize how often they were compensated for by many acts of simple courage, goodwill or resigna-tion.

Complete villains are rare, and most of those I have encountered were unfortunately out of my reach, outside our sphere of activity.

As for the others, I have done my best to prevent them from causing too much harm and to make sure that they pay for what they have done.

Once they do, I think the score has been settled.

There is no reason to come back to it.

8.

Place des Vosges, a young lady who is going to get married and Madame Maigret's little papers

'When it comes down to it,' Louise said, 'I don't see so much difference.'

I always look at her rather anxiously when she reads what I have just written, prepared to reply in advance to the objections she will make.

'Difference between what?'

'Between what you say about yourself and what Simenon says.'

'Oh!'

'Maybe I'm wrong to give my opinion.'

'Not at all!'

All the same, if she is right, I have gone to a lot of trouble for no purpose. And it is quite possible that she is right, that I have gone about it the wrong way and have not presented things as I vowed I would.

Or else that famous speech about fabricated truths being truer than naked truths is not just a paradox.

I have done my best. Only, there are a whole heap of things that seemed to me essential at first, points I had vowed to develop and which I abandoned as I went on.

For example, there is one whole shelf of my bookcase devoted to Simenon's books, which I have patiently annotated in blue pencil, and I was looking forward to rectifying all the errors he made, either because he did not know, or in order to increase the picturesque aspect – or, often, because he did not have the courage to call me and check a detail.

But what would be the point? That would make me look like a pernickety old man, and I too am starting to think that it does not really matter.

One of the things that has most irritated me from time to time is his habit of mixing up dates, of putting at the beginning of my career investigations that took place later, and vice versa, so that sometimes my inspectors are quite young when in fact they already had families and had settled down at the period in question, or the opposite.

I even intended – I can admit it now that I have given up the idea – to establish a chronology of the main cases in which I have been involved, with the help of the exercise books filled with press cuttings that my wife has been keeping up to date.

'Why not?' Simenon replied. 'Excellent idea. My books could be corrected for the next edition.'

He added without any irony:

'Only, my dear Maigret, you'll have to be so kind as to do the work yourself. I've never had the courage to reread my books.'

In short, I have said what I had to say, and too bad if I have not said it well. My colleagues will understand, and all those who are more or less in the trade. It was for them above all that I was determined to get things right, to speak not so much about myself as about our profession.

But apparently I have neglected an important question. I hear my wife carefully open the door of the dining room, where I am working, and tiptoe in.

She has just placed a little piece of paper on the table, before leaving as stealthily as she entered.

I read, in pencil: *Place des Vosges.*

And I cannot help smiling to myself with a sense of satisfaction, because it proves that she too has details to rectify, or at least one – and for the same reason as me, when it comes down to it: fidelity.

In her case, it is fidelity to our apartment on Boulevard Richard-Lenoir, which we have never abandoned, and which we still have, even though we have only used it for a few days a year since we moved to the country.

In several of his books, Simenon had us living on Place des Vosges without giving any explanation.

I am therefore carrying out my wife's request. Yes, we did live on Place des Vosges for a few months. But we were not there with our own furniture.

That year, our landlord finally made up his mind to undertake the refurbishment the building had needed for a long time. Workers set up scaffolding on the façade, enclosing our windows. Inside, others started breaking through walls and floors in order to install central heating. We were promised it would all take three weeks at most. After two weeks, they had got nowhere. Just then, a strike was declared in the building trade, and it was impossible to predict how long it would last.

Simenon was leaving for Africa, where he would spend nearly a year.

'Why don't you come and live in my apartment on Place des Vosges until the work is finished?'

That is how we came to live there, at Number 21, to be precise, and nobody could have accused us of being disloyal to our good old boulevard.

There was also a time when, without telling me in advance, he retired me, even though I was still several years away from retirement.

We had just bought our house in Meung-sur-Loire, and we spent every free Sunday I had doing it up. He came to see us there. He liked the place so much that in the next book he anticipated events, shamelessly aged me and settled me there for good.

'It makes a nice change of scenery,' he said when I spoke to him about it. '*I was starting to get tired of Quai des Orfèvres.*'

I find that sentence extraordinary, which is why I have put it in italics. It was *he*, you understand, who was starting to get tired of the Quai, of *my* office, of the daily work of the Police Judiciaire!

Which did not prevent him subsequently, and will probably not prevent him in the future, from writing about older investigations, always without providing dates, sometimes making me sixty, sometimes forty-five.

My wife again. I do not have an office here. I have no need of one. Whenever I want to work, I sit down at the dining-room table, and Louise just has to stay in the kitchen, which she does not mind. I look at her, assuming that she wants to say something. But she is holding another piece of paper, which she timidly puts down in front of me.

A list this time, as when I go to town and she writes what she wants me to bring back for her on a page torn out of a notebook.

My nephew is top of the list, and I understand why. He is her sister's son. I helped him to join the police, at an age when he thought he had a vocation.

Simenon wrote about him, then the boy suddenly vanished from his books, and I understand Louise's qualms. She must be thinking that some readers may have found this odd, as if her nephew had done something stupid.

The truth is quite simple. He was not as brilliant as he had hoped. And he did not long resist the urging of his father-in-law, a soap manufacturer, who offered him a job in his factory.

Next on the list is Torrence, fat Torrence, noisy Torrence (I think Simenon once killed him off instead of another inspector, who was actually killed by my side in a hotel on the Champs-Élysées).

Torrence did not have a father-in-law in soap. But he did have a great appetite for life as well as a feeling for business that was not really compatible with the life of a civil servant.

He left us to start a private detective agency – a perfectly serious agency, I hasten to add, because such is not always the case. And for a long time he continued coming to the Quai to ask us for help, a piece of information, or simply to breathe the air of the house for a while.

He owns a big American car, which stops from time to time outside our door and each time he is accompanied by a pretty woman, never the same one, whom he introduces in all sincerity as his fiancée.

I read the third name: young Janvier, as we have always called him. He is still at the Quai. No doubt they still call him young.

In his last letter, he announced to me, not without a certain sadness, that his daughter is about to marry a former student of the École Polytechnique.

Last but not least, Lucas, at this hour, is probably sitting as usual in my office, in my place, smoking one of my pipes, which he asked me with tears in his eyes to leave him as a memento.

There are two more words at the bottom of the list. I thought at first it was a name, but I cannot read it.

I have just been all the way to the kitchen, which I was quite surprised to see bathed in bright sunshine, because I had closed the shutters to work in the kind of half-light I find congenial.

'Finished?'

'No. There are some words I can't read.'

She was quite embarrassed. 'It doesn't matter.'

'What is it?'

'Nothing. Don't pay any attention.'

Of course I insisted.

'The sloe gin!' she finally admitted, turning away her head.

She knew I was going to burst out laughing, and I did not fail her.

When it came to my famous bowler hat, my overcoat with the velvet collar, my coal stove and my poker, I knew she found my insistence on setting the record straight somewhat childish.

Nevertheless, she scribbled the words 'sloe gin' at the bottom of the list, deliberately making them illegible, I'm sure, out of a kind of shame – rather as when she adds a very feminine article to the list of errands to be run in town, an article she feels embarrassed asking me to buy.

Simenon has written about a certain drink, a bottle of which was always on the dresser in the apartment on Boulevard Richard-Lenoir – and is now here. My sister-in-law, following a tradition that has become sacred, brings us a supply from Alsace on her annual visit.

He wrote carelessly that it was sloe gin.

In fact, it is raspberry liqueur. For someone from Alsace, there is apparently a very big difference.

'I've rectified it, Louise. Your sister will be pleased.'

This time I left the kitchen door open.

'Anything else?'

'Tell Simenon I'm just knitting some bootees for—'

'Come on now, this isn't a letter!'

'That's true. Make a note of it for when you write to them. And make sure they don't forget the photograph they promised.'

Then she added:

'Can I lay the table?'

And that is all.

OTHER TITLES IN THE SERIES

THE CELLARS OF THE MAJESTIC
GEORGES SIMENON

'Try to imagine a guest, a wealthy woman, staying at the Majestic with her husband, her son, a nurse and a governess... At six in the morning, she's strangled, not in her room, but in the basement locker room.'

Below stairs at a glamorous hotel on the Champs-Élysèes, the workers' lives are worlds away from the luxury enjoyed by the wealthy guests. When their worlds meet, Maigret discovers a tragic story of ambition, blackmail and unrequited love.

Translated by Howard Curtis

OTHER TITLES IN THE SERIES

THE JUDGE'S HOUSE
GEORGES SIMENON

'He went out, lit his pipe and walked slowly to the harbour. He could hear scurrying footsteps behind him. The sea was becoming swollen. The beams of the lighthouses joined in the sky. The moon had just risen and the judge's house emerged from the darkness, all white, a crude, livid, unreal white.'

Exiled from the Police Judiciare in Paris, Maigret bides his time in a remote coastal town in France. There, among the lighthouses, mussel farms and the eerie wail of foghorns, he discovers that a community's loyalties hide unpleasant truths.

Translated by Howard Curtis

OTHER TITLES IN THE SERIES

SIGNED, PICPUS
GEORGES SIMENON

'"It's a matter of life and death!" he said.

A small, thin man, rather dull to look at, neither young nor old, exuding the stale smell of a bachelor who does not look after himself. He pulls his fingers and cracks his knuckles while telling his tale, the way a schoolboy recites his lesson.'

A mysterious note predicting the murder of a fortune-teller; a confused old man locked in a Paris apartment; a financier who goes fishing; a South American heiress... Maigret must make his way through a frustrating maze of clues, suspects and motives to find out what connects them.

Translated by David Coward

INSPECTOR MAIGRET

OTHER TITLES IN THE SERIES

INSPECTOR CADAVER
GEORGES SIMENON

'To everyone, even the old ladies hiding behind their quivering curtains, even the kids just now who had turned to stare after they had passed him, he was the intruder, the undesirable.'

Asked to help a friend in trouble, Maigret arrives in a small provincial town where curtains twitch and gossip is rife. He also finds himself facing an unexpected adversary: the pale, shifty ex-policeman they call 'Inspector Cadaver'.

Translated by William Hobson

OTHER TITLES IN THE SERIES

FÉLICIE
GEORGES SIMENON

'In his mind's eye he would see that slim figure in the striking clothes, those wide eyes the colour of forget-me-not, the pert nose and especially the hat, that giddy, crimson bonnet perched on the top of her head with a bronze-green feather shaped like a blade stuck in it.'

Investigating the death of a retired sailor on the outskirts of Paris, Maigret meets his match in the form of the old man's housekeeper: the sharp-witted, enigmatic and elusive Félicie.

Translated by David Coward

OTHER TITLES IN THE SERIES

www.penguin.com